There's matter in these sighs, these profound heaves.
You must translate: 'tis fit we understand them.

(*Hamlet*, 4.1.1–2)

D0980447

FEAR NOT.

Have you ever found yourself looking at a Shakespeare play, then down at the footnotes, then back at the play, and still not understanding? You know what the individual words mean, but they don't add up. SparkNotes' *No Fear Shakespeare* will help you break through all that. Put the pieces together with our easy-to-read translations. Soon you'll be reading Shakespeare's own words fearlessly—and actually enjoying it.

No Fear Shakespeare puts Shakespeare's language side-by-side with a facing-page translation into modern English— the kind of English people actually speak today. When Shakespeare's words make your head spin, our translation will help you sort out what's happening, who's saying what, and why.

v

NO FEAR SHAKESPEARE

NO FEAR SHAKESPEARE

NO FEAR SHAKESPEARE

OTHELLO

SPARK NOTES

SPARKNOTES is a registered trademark of SparkNotes LLC.

Spark Publishing
A Division of Barnes & Noble, Inc.
120 Fifth Avenue
New York, NY 10011
www.sparknotes.com

Please submit all comments and questions or report errors to www.sparknotes.com/errors

ISBN: 978-1-5866-3852-8

Library of Congress Cataloging-in-Publication Data

Shakespeare, William, 1564–1616.
Othello / edited by John Crowther.
    p. cm.—(No fear Shakespeare)
  Summary: Presents the original text of Shakespeare's play side by side with a modern
version, with marginal notes and explanations and full descriptions of each character.
  ISBN 1-58663-852-1 (pbk.) ISBN 1-4114-0050-X (hc.)
  1. Othello (Fictitious character)—Drama. 2. Venice (Italy)—Fiction. 3. Jealousy—Drama.
4.Muslims—Drama. [1. Shakespeare, William, 1564–1616. Othello. 2. Plays. 3. English
literature—History and criticism.]
  I. Crowther, John (John C.) II. Title.
PR2829 .A2 C74 2003
822.3'3—dc22

                                         2003015664

Printed and bound in the United States of America

50 49 48 47 46 45 44 43 42 41

OTHELLO

CHARACTERS

Othello—The play's protagonist and hero. Othello is the highly respected general of the armies of Venice, although he is not a native of Venice but rather a Moor, or North African. He is an eloquent and powerful figure, respected by all those around him. In spite of his elevated status, Othello is nevertheless easy prey to insecurities because of his age, his life as a soldier, and his self-consciousness about being a racial and cultural outsider. He possesses a free and open nature that his ensign Iago exploits to twist Othello's love for his wife, Desdemona, into a powerful and destructive jealousy.

Desdemona—The daughter of the Venetian senator Brabantio. Desdemona and Othello are secretly married before the play begins. While in some ways stereotypically pure and meek, Desdemona is also determined and self-possessed. She is equally capable of defending her marriage, jesting bawdily with Iago, and responding with dignity to Othello's incomprehensible jealousy.

Iago—Othello's ensign (a senior position also known as "ancient" or "standard-bearer"), a twenty-eight-year-old military veteran from Venice. Iago is the villain of the play. Although he is obsessive, relentless, bold, and ingenius in his efforts to manipulate and deceive the other characters—particularly Othello—Iago's motivations are notoriously murky. At various points in the play, he claims to be motivated by different things: resentment that Othello passed him over for a promotion in favor of Michael Cassio; jealousy because he heard a rumor that Othello slept with Iago's wife, Emilia; suspicion that Cassio slept with Emilia too. Iago gives the impression that he's tossing out plausible motivations as he thinks of them, and that we'll never understand what really drives his villainy. He hates women and is obsessed with other people's sex lives.

Michael Cassio—Othello's lieutenant, or second-in-command. Cassio is highly educated but young and inexperienced in battle. Iago resents Cassio's high position and dismisses him as a bookkeeper. Truly devoted to Othello, Cassio is ashamed after being implicated in a drunken brawl on Cyprus and losing his place as lieutenant. Iago uses Cassio's youth, good looks, and flirtatious manner with women to play on Othello's insecurities about Desdemona's fidelity.

Emilia—Iago's wife and Desdemona's attendant. A cynical, worldly woman, Emilia is deeply attached to her mistress and distrustful of her husband.

Roderigo—A jealous suitor of Desdemona. Young, rich, and foolish, Roderigo is convinced that if he gives Iago all of his money, Iago will help him win Desdemona's hand. Repeatedly frustrated as Othello marries Desdemona and then takes her to Cyprus, Roderigo is ultimately desperate enough to agree to help Iago kill Cassio after Iago points out that Cassio is another potential rival for Desdemona.

Bianca—A courtesan, or prostitute, in Cyprus. Bianca's favorite customer is Cassio, who teases her with promises of marriage but laughs at her behind her back.

Brabantio—Desdemona's father, a somewhat blustering and self-important Venetian senator. As a friend of Othello, Brabantio feels betrayed when the general marries his daughter in secret.

Duke of Venice—The official authority in Venice, the duke has great respect for Othello as a public and military servant. His primary role within the play is to make Othello tell his story of how he wooed Desdemona, and then to send Othello to Cyprus.

Montano—The governor of Cyprus before Othello. We see Montano first in Act Two, as he recounts the status of the war and awaits the Venetian ships.

Lodovico—One of Brabantio's kinsmen, Lodovico acts as a messenger from Venice to Cyprus. He arrives in Cyprus in Act Four with letters announcing that Cassio is to replace Othello as governor.

Graziano—Brabantio's kinsman who accompanies Lodovico to Cyprus. Amidst the chaos of the play's final scene, Graziano mentions that Desdemona's father has died.

Clown—Othello's servant. Although the clown appears only in two short scenes, his jokes reflect and distort the action and words of the main plots: his puns on the word "lie" in Act Three, scene 4, for example, anticipate Othello's confusion of two meanings of that word in Act Four, scene 1.

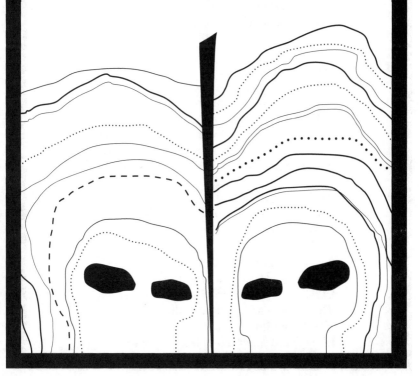

NO FEAR SHAKESPEARE

OTHELLO

ACT ONE

SCENE 1

Enter RODERIGO *and* IAGO

RODERIGO

Tush! Never tell me. I take it much unkindly
That thou, Iago, who hast had my purse
As if the strings were thine, shouldst know of this.

IAGO

'Sblood, but you'll not hear me! If ever I did dream
5   of such a matter, abhor me.

RODERIGO

Thou told'st me
Thou didst hold him in thy hate.

IAGO

Despise me
If I do not. Three great ones of the city
10   (In personal suit to make me his lieutenant)
Off-capped to him, and by the faith of man
I know my price, I am worth no worse a place.
But he (as loving his own pride and purposes)
Evades them with a bombast circumstance
15   Horribly stuffed with epithets of war,
And in conclusion
Nonsuits my mediators. For "Certes," says he,
"I have already chose my officer."
And what was he?
20   Forsooth, a great arithmetician, Math
One Michael Cassio, a Florentine
(A fellow almost damned in a fair wife)
That never set a squadron in the field,
Nor the division of a battle knows
25   More than a spinster—unless the bookish theoric,

ACT ONE
SCENE 1

RODERIGO *and* IAGO *enter.*

RODERIGO

Come on, don't tell me that. I don't like it that you knew about this, Iago. All this time I've thought you were such a good friend that I've let you spend my money as if it were yours.

IAGO

Damn it, you're not listening to me! I never dreamed this was happening—if you find out I did, you can go ahead and hate me.

RODERIGO

You told me you hated him.

IAGO

They're talking about Othello, though they never mention his name.

I do hate him, I swear. Three of Venice's most important noblemen took their hats off to him and asked him humbly to make me his lieutenant, the second in command. And I know my own worth well enough to know I deserve that position. But he wants to have things his own way, so he sidesteps the issue with a lot of military talk and refuses their request. "I've already chosen my lieutenant," he says. And who does he choose? A guy who knows more about numbers then fighting! This guy from Florence named Michael Cassio. He has a pretty wife but he can't even control her. And he's definitely never commanded men in battle. He's got no more hands-on knowledge of warfare than an old woman—unless you count what he's read in books,

Wherein the toged consuls can propose
As masterly as he. Mere prattle without practice
Is all his soldiership. But he, sir, had th' election
And I, of whom his eyes had seen the proof
30 At Rhodes, at Cyprus, and on other grounds
Christian and heathen, must be belee'd and calmed
By debitor and creditor. This counter-caster
He (in good time) must his lieutenant be
And I, bless the mark, his Moorship's ancient.

RODERIGO
35 By heaven, I rather would have been his hangman.

IAGO
Why, there's no remedy. 'Tis the curse of service.
Preferment goes by letter and affection,
And not by old gradation, where each second
Stood heir to th' first. Now sir, be judge yourself,
40 Whether I in any just term am affined
To love the Moor.

RODERIGO
I would not follow him then.

IAGO
O sir, content you.
I follow him to serve my turn upon him.
45 We cannot all be masters, nor all masters
Cannot be truly followed. You shall mark
Many a duteous and knee-crooking knave
That (doting on his own obsequious bondage)
Wears out his time much like his master's ass
50 For naught but provender, and when he's old, cashiered.
Whip me such honest knaves. Others there are
Who, trimmed in forms and visages of duty,
Keep yet their hearts attending on themselves
And, throwing but shows of service on their lords,
55 Do well thrive by them. And when they have lined their
coats,
Do themselves homage. These fellows have some soul,

which any peace-lover can do. His military under-standing is all theory, no practice. But Cassio's been chosen over me. My career is cut short by some book-keeper, even though the general saw my fighting skills first-hand in Rhodes and Cyprus. This accountant is now lieutenant, while I end up as the Moor's flag-bearer.

Moor = North African

RODERIGO

By God, I'd rather be his executioner.

IAGO

And there's nothing I can do about it. That's the curse of military service. You get promoted when someone likes you, not because you're next in line. Now, you tell me: should I feel loyal to the Moor?

RODERIGO

If you don't like him you should quit.

IAGO

No, calm down. I'm serving under him to take advan-tage of him. We can't all be masters, and not all mas-ters should be followed. Look at all the devoted servants who work for their masters their whole lives for nothing but their food, and then when they get old they're terminated. They ought to be whipped for being so stupid. But then there's another kind of ser-vant who looks dutiful and devoted, but who's really looking out for himself. By pretending to serve their lords, these men get rich, and when they've saved up enough they can be their own masters. Guys like that have soul, and that's the kind of guy I am. Let me tell

And such a one do I profess myself. For, sir,
It is as sure as you are Roderigo,
Were I the Moor, I would not be Iago.
60 In following him, I follow but myself.
Heaven is my judge, not I for love and duty,
But seeming so, for my peculiar end.
For when my outward action doth demonstrate
The native act and figure of my heart
65 In compliment extern, 'tis not long after
But I will wear my heart upon my sleeve
For daws to peck at. I am not what I am.

RODERIGO

What a full fortune does the Thick-lips owe
If he can carry't thus!

IAGO

                              Call up her father.
70 Rouse him. Make after him, Poison his delight,
Proclaim him in the streets. Incense her kinsmen,
And, though he in a fertile climate dwell,
Plague him with flies. Though that his joy be joy
Yet throw such changes of vexation on't,
75 As it may lose some color.

RODERIGO

Here is her father's house, I'll call aloud.

IAGO

Do, with like timorous accent and dire yell
As when, by night and negligence, the fire
Is spied in populous cities.

RODERIGO

80 What, ho, Brabantio! Signior Brabantio, ho!

IAGO

Awake! What, ho, Brabantio! Thieves! Thieves!
Look to your house, your daughter, and your bags!
Thieves! thieves!

Enter BRABANTIO, *above*

you, as sure as your name's Roderigo, if I were the Moor I wouldn't want to be Iago. I may seem to love and obey him, but in fact, I'm just serving him to get what I want. If my outward appearance started reflecting what I really felt, soon enough I'd be wearing my heart on my sleeve for birds to peck at. No, it's better to hide it. I'm not who I appear to be.

RODERIGO

"Thick-lips" is a racial slur toward the Moor, Othello.

Thick-lips sure is lucky if he can pull this off!

IAGO

Let's shout up to Desdemona's father, wake him, pester him, spoil his happiness, spread rumors about him in the streets, enrage his relatives, and irritate him endlessly. However real his happiness is, it will vanish in light of this.

RODERIGO

Here's her father's house. I'll call out.

IAGO

Do it, and shout like the city's on fire.

RODERIGO

Hey, Brabantio! Signor Brabantio, hey!

IAGO

Wake up, Brabantio! Wake up! Thieves! Thieves! Check on your daughter, your house, your money! Thieves! Thieves!

BRABANTIO *enters, above.*

BRABANTIO
What is the reason of this terrible summons?
85   What is the matter there?

RODERIGO
Signior, is all your family within?

IAGO
Are your doors locked?

BRABANTIO
                  Why, wherefore ask you this?

IAGO
Zounds, sir, you're robbed! For shame, put on your gown.
Your heart is burst, you have lost half your soul.
90   Even now, now, very now, an old black ram
Is tupping your white ewe. Arise, arise,
Awake the snorting citizens with the bell
Or else the devil will make a grandsire of you.
Arise, I say!

BRABANTIO
              What, have you lost your wits?

RODERIGO
95   Most reverend signior, do you know my voice?

BRABANTIO
Not I. What are you?

RODERIGO
My name is Roderigo.

BRABANTIO
The worser welcome.
I have charged thee not to haunt about my doors.
100   In honest plainness thou hast heard me say
My daughter is not for thee. And now in madness,
Being full of supper and distempering drafts,
Upon malicious knavery dost thou come
To start my quiet?

RODERIGO
105   Sir, sir, sir—

BRABANTIO

What's the reason for this horrible shouting? What's the matter?

RODERIGO

Sir, is everyone in your family at home?

IAGO

Are your doors locked?

BRABANTIO

Why are you asking me that?

IAGO

For God's sake, sir, you've been robbed. Get dressed. Your heart's going to break. It's like half your soul's been ripped out. At this very minute an old black ram is having sex with your little white lamb. Wake up, wake up, ring a bell and wake up all the snoring citizens. If you wait too long you'll have black grand-children. Get up, I tell you!

BRABANTIO

Are you crazy?

RODERIGO

Do you recognize my voice, noble lord?

BRABANTIO

Not me. Who are you?

RODERIGO

My name's Roderigo.

BRABANTIO

I told you not to hang around my house. I've already told you quite plainly that my daughter will never marry you. Now you come here drunk to make trouble and startle me out of a sound sleep?

RODERIGO

Sir, sir, sir—

BRABANTIO
But thou must needs be sure
My spirits and my place have in their power
To make this bitter to thee.

RODERIGO
Patience, good sir.

BRABANTIO
What tell'st thou me of robbing? This is Venice,
110   My house is not a grange.

RODERIGO
Most grave Brabantio,
In simple and pure soul I come to you—

IAGO
Zounds, sir, you are one of those that will not serve God,
if the devil bid you. Because we come to do you service and
you think we are ruffians, you'll have your daughter
115   covered with a Barbary horse. You'll have your nephews
neigh to you. You'll have coursers for cousins and gennets
for germans.

BRABANTIO
What profane wretch art thou?

IAGO
I am one, sir, that comes to tell you your daughter
120   and the Moor are now making the beast with two backs.

BRABANTIO
Thou art a villain!

IAGO
You are a senator!

BRABANTIO
This thou shalt answer. I know thee, Roderigo.

RODERIGO
Sir, I will answer any thing. But, I beseech you,
If't be your pleasure and most wise consent
125   (As partly I find it is) that your fair daughter
At this odd-even and dull watch o' th' night
Transported with no worse nor better guard

BRABANTIO

You know I'm powerful enough to make you pay for this.

RODERIGO

Please wait, sir.

BRABANTIO

Why are you talking about robbery? This is Venice. My house isn't in some remote countryside.

RODERIGO

Brabantio, with all due respect, I'm here out of courtesy and good will. I've come to tell you—

IAGO

My God, sir, you're stubborn and suspicious. We come here to help you and you treat us like thugs, but you let an African horse climb all over your daughter. Your grandsons will neigh to you like horses. Your whole family will be ruined.

BRABANTIO

What kind of crude jerk are you?

IAGO

The kind that tells you that the Moor is having sex with your daughter right now.

BRABANTIO

You're a villain!

IAGO

You're a senator!

BRABANTIO

You're going to pay for this, Roderigo. I know who you are.

RODERIGO

I'll answer for everything. I don't know if you know or approve of this, but in the wee hours of the morning your daughter left your house, with no better escort than a hired gondolier, to go into the rough embrace of a lustful Moor. If all of this happened with your

But with a knave of common hire, a gondolier,
To the gross clasps of a lascivious Moor,
130   If this be known to you and your allowance,
We then have done you bold and saucy wrongs.
But if you know not this my manners tell me
We have your wrong rebuke. Do not believe
That, from the sense of all civility,
135   I thus would play and trifle with your reverence.
Your daughter (if you have not given her leave)
I say again, hath made a gross revolt,
Tying her duty, beauty, wit, and fortunes
In an extravagant and wheeling stranger
140   Of here and everywhere. Straight satisfy yourself.
If she be in her chamber or your house,
Let loose on me the justice of the state
For thus deluding you.

BRABANTIO

Strike on the tinder, ho!
Give me a taper, call up all my people!
145   This accident is not unlike my dream,
Belief of it oppresses me already.
Light, I say, light!

Exit above

IAGO

(to RODERIGO*)*

Farewell, for I must leave you.
It seems not meet, nor wholesome to my place,
To be producted (as, if I stay, I shall)
150   Against the Moor. For I do know the state
(However this may gall him with some check)
Cannot with safety cast him, for he's embarked
With such loud reason to the Cyprus wars
(Which even now stand in act) that, for their souls,
155   Another of his fathom they have none
To lead their business. In which regard,
Though I do hate him as I do hell pains,

approval, then we've been very rude to bother you like this. But if you didn't know about it, then you were wrong to get mad at us. I'd never play pranks on you. If you didn't allow your daughter to do what she's doing, then she's rebelling against you. She's throwing her life away on some stranger. Go ahead, see for yourself if she's in her bedroom. If she is, you can sue me for lying to you.

BRABANTIO

Light the candles! Wake up my whole household! I dreamt about this. I'm starting to worry it's true. Give me some light!

BRABANTIO exits.

IAGO

(to RODERIGO) It's time for me to say goodbye to you. It would be inappropriate—dangerous, even—for me to be seen working against the Moor, as I would if I stayed. The Venetian government might reprimand him for this, but it can't safely get rid of him, since it needs him urgently for the imminent Cyprus wars. They couldn't find another man with his abilities to lead their armed forces—not if their souls depended on it. I hate him, but I've got to show him signs of loy-

Yet for necessity of present life
I must show out a flag and sign of love,
160   (Which is indeed but sign). That you shall surely find him,
Lead to the Sagittary the raisèd search,
And there will I be with him. So farewell.

Exit

Enter BRABANTIO, *with servants and torches*

BRABANTIO
It is too true an evil. Gone she is.
And what's to come of my despisèd time
165   Is naught but bitterness. Now, Roderigo,
Where didst thou see her?—Oh, unhappy girl!—
With the Moor, say'st thou?—Who would be a father?—
How didst thou know 'twas she?—Oh, she deceives me
Past thought!—What said she to you?—Get more tapers,
170   Raise all my kindred. Are they married, think you?

RODERIGO
Truly, I think they are.

BRABANTIO
Oh, heaven, how got she out? Oh, treason of the blood!
Fathers, from hence trust not your daughters' minds
By what you see them act. Is there not charms
175   By which the property of youth and maidhood
May be abused? Have you not read, Roderigo,
Of some such thing?

RODERIGO
                              Yes, sir, I have indeed.

BRABANTIO
Call up my brother—Oh, would you had had her!
Some one way, some another. Do you know
180   Where we may apprehend her and the Moor?

RODERIGO
I think I can discover him, if you please
To get good guard and go along with me.

alty and affection, even if it's just an act. If you want to find him, send the search party to the Sagittarius Inn. He and I will be there.

IAGO *exits.*

BRABANTIO *enters with servants and torches.*

BRABANTIO

It's true. She's gone. The rest of my life will be nothing but bitterness. Now, Roderigo, where did you see her?—Oh, that miserable wretch!—You say you saw her with the Moor?—Oh, who would want to be a father?—How did you know it was her?—To think she tricked me so easily!—What did she say to you?— Get me more candles, and wake up all my relatives. Do you think they're married?

RODERIGO

Yes, I really think so.

BRABANTIO

Oh, heaven, how did she get out? My own flesh and blood rebels against me! Fathers, never trust your daughters just because they act obedient and inno-cent. Are there magic spells that can lead young vir-gins astray? Have you ever heard of anything like that, Roderigo?

RODERIGO

Yes, sir, I have.

BRABANTIO

Call my brother.—Now I wish you'd married her!— Some of you go one way, some the other way.—Do you know where we can find her and the Moor?

RODERIGO

I think I can find him. Get together a group of armed men and follow me.

BRABANTIO
Pray you lead on. At every house I'll call.
I may command at most.—Get weapons, ho!
185   And raise some special officers of might.—
On, good Roderigo. I will deserve your pains.

Exeunt

BRABANTIO

> Lead the way. I'll stop at every house. I'm respected enough that most of them will do what I say.—Get your weapons! And get the officers who guard the city at night.—Let's go, Roderigo. I'll reward you for your troubles.

They exit.

ACT 1, SCENE 2

Enter OTHELLO, IAGO, *and attendants with torches*

IAGO

Though in the trade of war I have slain men,
Yet do I hold it very stuff o' th' conscience
To do no contrived murder. I lack iniquity
Sometimes to do me service. Nine or ten times
5   I had thought t' have yerked him here under the ribs.

OTHELLO

'Tis better as it is.

IAGO

              Nay, but he prated
And spoke such scurvy and provoking terms
Against your honor
That, with the little godliness I have,
10   I did full hard forbear him. But I pray you, sir,
Are you fast married? Be assured of this:
That the Magnifico is much beloved
And hath in his effect a voice potential
As double as the Duke's. He will divorce you,
15   Or put upon you what restraint and grievance
The law (with all his might to enforce it on)
Will give him cable.

OTHELLO

              Let him do his spite.
My services which I have done the signiory
Shall out-tongue his complaints. 'Tis yet to know—
20   Which, when I know that boasting is an honor,
I shall promulgate. I fetch my life and being
From men of royal siege, and my demerits
May speak unbonneted to as proud a fortune
As this that I have reached. For know, Iago,
25   But that I love the gentle Desdemona,
I would not my unhousèd free condition
Put into circumscription and confine
For the sea's worth. But look, what lights come yond?

ACT 1, SCENE 2

OTHELLO *and* IAGO *enter, followed by attendants with torches.*

IAGO

I've killed many men in battle, but I still believe it's deeply wrong to murder someone. Sometimes I worry I'm not cruel enough for this job. Nine or ten times I wanted to stab him under the ribs.

OTHELLO

It's better that you didn't kill him.

IAGO

But he kept chattering so foolishly, talking about you in such insulting and despicable terms, that it was hard for me to restrain myself. But please tell me, sir, is your marriage secure? Brabantio is an important man in this city, almost as powerful as the duke himself. He'll try to annul your marriage, or else inflict whatever punishment the law and his power will allow him to.

Iago may be asking whether Othello has consummated his marriage by sleeping with Desdemona yet. A marriage could be annulled if it had never been consummated.

OTHELLO

Let him do his worst. The services I have done for the Venetian government will count for more than his complaints will. No one knows this yet—and I don't like to brag, but I come from a royal family, and I'm as noble as the woman I've married. And let me tell you, Iago, if I didn't love Desdemona as much as I do, I'd never agree to get married and lose my freedom at all. But look at those lights. Who's coming?

IAGO

Those are the raisèd father and his friends.

30   You were best go in.

OTHELLO

                Not I, I must be found.

My parts, my title, and my perfect soul

Shall manifest me rightly. Is it they?

IAGO

By Janus, I think no.

Enter CASSIO, *with officers and torches*

OTHELLO

The servants of the Duke and my lieutenant?

35   The goodness of the night upon you, friends!

What is the news?

CASSIO

            The Duke does greet you, general,

And he requires your haste-post-haste appearance,

Even on the instant.

OTHELLO

             What's the matter, think you?

CASSIO

Something from Cyprus as I may divine.

40   It is a business of some heat. The galleys

Have sent a dozen sequent messengers

This very night at one another's heels,

And many of the consuls, raised and met,

Are at the Duke's already. You have been hotly called for.

45   When being not at your lodging to be found

The Senate hath sent about three several guests

To search you out.

OTHELLO

           'Tis well I am found by you.

I will but spend a word here in the house

And go with you.

IAGO

That's her father and his friends, who've been roused out of bed. You'd better go inside.

OTHELLO

No, I must let them find me. My good qualities, my legal status as Desdemona's husband, and my innocence will protect me. Is it them?

IAGO

I don't think so.

CASSIO *enters with officers and men carrying torches.*

OTHELLO

The servants of the Duke and my lieutenant? Hello, everyone! What's going on?

CASSIO

The Duke sends his regards. He needs to see you right away.

OTHELLO

What do you think he wants?

CASSIO

Something about Cyprus. I think it's important. The warships have sent a dozen messages tonight, one after the other, and many of the senators have been awakened and are at the Duke's already. They're very anxious for you to get there. When you weren't at home, the Senate sent out three different search parties to find you.

OTHELLO

It's good you found me. I'll just speak a word or two here in the house and then I'll go with you.

Exit

CASSIO

Ancient, what makes he here?

IAGO

50 Faith, he tonight hath boarded a land carrack.
If it prove lawful prize, he's made for ever.

CASSIO

I do not understand.

IAGO

He's married.

CASSIO

To who?

IAGO

Marry, to—

Enter OTHELLO

Come, captain, will you go?

OTHELLO

55 Have with you.

CASSIO

Here comes another troop to seek for you.

Enter BRABANTIO, RODERIGO, *and officers with torches and
weapons*

IAGO

It is Brabantio. General, be advised,
He comes to bad intent.

OTHELLO

Holla! Stand there!

RODERIGO

Signior, it is the Moor.

BRABANTIO

Down with him, thief!

They draw their swords

OTHELLO *exits.*

CASSIO

Ensign, what's he doing in there?

IAGO

Tonight he boarded a treasure ship. If he can keep it, he'll be set forever.

CASSIO

I don't understand.

IAGO

He's married.

CASSIO

To whom?

IAGO

To—

OTHELLO *enters.*

Are you ready?

OTHELLO

Yes, I'll go with you now.

CASSIO

Here comes another group looking for you.

BRABANTIO *and* RODERIGO *enter, followed by* OFFICERS *and men with torches.*

IAGO

It's Brabantio. Look out, sir. He intends to do something bad to you.

OTHELLO

Hey! Stop right there!

RODERIGO

Sir, it's the Moor.

BRABANTIO

Get him, he's a thief!

Both sides draw their swords.

IAGO

60   You, Roderigo! Come, sir, I am for you.

OTHELLO

Keep up your bright swords, for the dew will rust them.
Good signior, you shall more command with years
Than with your weapons.

BRABANTIO

O thou foul thief, where hast thou stowed my daughter?
65   Damned as thou art, thou hast enchanted her!
For I'll refer me to all things of sense,
If she in chains of magic were not bound,
Whether a maid so tender, fair, and happy,
So opposite to marriage that she shunned
70   The wealthy curlèd darlings of our nation,
Would ever have, t' incur a general mock,
Run from her guardage to the sooty bosom
Of such a thing as thou—to fear, not to delight.
Judge me the world if 'tis not gross in sense
75   That thou hast practiced on her with foul charms,
Abused her delicate youth with drugs or minerals
That weakens motion. I'll have 't disputed on.
'Tis probable and palpable to thinking.
I therefore apprehend and do attach thee
80   For an abuser of the world, a practicer
Of arts inhibited and out of warrant.—
Lay hold upon him. If he do resist,
Subdue him at his peril!

OTHELLO

Hold your hands,
Both you of my inclining and the rest.
85   Were it my cue to fight, I should have known it
Without a prompter. Whither will you that I go
To answer this your charge?

IAGO

You, Roderigo! Come on, I'll fight you.

OTHELLO

Put away your swords. They'll get rusty in the dew. Sir, your age and status inspire more respect than your weapons do.

BRABANTIO

You evil thief, where have you hidden my daughter? You devil, you've put a spell on her! Anybody with eyes could tell you that a beautiful and happy young girl like her, who's refused to marry all of the handsome young men of the city, wouldn't run off with a black thing like you unless she'd been bewitched. You're something to fear, not to love. It's obvious to everyone that you've tricked her, drugged her, or kidnapped her. That's probably what happened, so I'm arresting you.—Arrest this man as a practitioner of black magic. Grab him. If he struggles, use force!

OTHELLO

Just a minute. I don't need anyone to tell me when to fight. You've accused me of some serious crimes. Where do you want me to go to respond to these charges?

BRABANTIO

                                        To prison, till fit time
Of law and course of direct session
Call thee to answer.

OTHELLO

                                        What if I do obey?
How may the Duke be therewith satisfied,
Whose messengers are here about my side
Upon some present business of the state
To bring me to him?

OFFICER

                                        'Tis true, most worthy signior.
The Duke's in council and your noble self,
I am sure, is sent for.

BRABANTIO

                                        How? The Duke in council?
In this time of the night? Bring him away.
Mine's not an idle cause. The Duke himself,
Or any of my brothers of the state,
Cannot but feel this wrong as 'twere their own.
For if such actions may have passage free,
Bond-slaves and pagans shall our statesmen be.

                                                        Exeunt

BRABANTIO

> To prison, until you're called into court.

OTHELLO

> What if I do what you say? How would I satisfy the Duke then? His messengers are waiting here to take me to him immediately, on pressing state business.

OFFICER

> It's true. The Duke's in a meeting right now, and he's sent for you too.

BRABANTIO

> The Duke's in a meeting? At this time of night? Bring him with us. The law's on my side. The Duke and any of my fellow senators will take this wrong as seriously as if it were their own. If we let crimes like this happen, slaves and heathens will be our rulers.

They all exit.

ACT 1, SCENE 3

Enter DUKE, SENATORS, *and* OFFICERS

DUKE
> There's no composition in this news
> That gives them credit.

FIRST SENATOR
> Indeed, they are disproportioned.
> My letters say a hundred and seven galleys.

DUKE
5   And mine a hundred and forty.

SECOND SENATOR
>   And mine, two hundred.
> But though they jump not on a just account—
> As in these cases, where the aim reports
> 'Tis oft with difference—yet do they all confirm
> A Turkish fleet, and bearing up to Cyprus.

DUKE
10   Nay, it is possible enough to judgment.
> I do not so secure me in the error,
> But the main article I do approve
> In fearful sense.

SAILOR
> *(within)*
>   What, ho, what, ho, what, ho!

OFFICER
> A messenger from the galleys.

Enter SAILOR

DUKE
15   Now, what's the business?

SAILOR
> The Turkish preparation makes for Rhodes,
> So was I bid report here to the state
> By Signior Angelo.

ACT 1, SCENE 3

The DUKE *enters with* SENATORS *and* OFFICERS.

DUKE

These reports are inconsistent. You can't trust them.

FIRST SENATOR

It's true, they're inconsistent. My letters say there are a hundred and seven ships.

DUKE

And mine say a hundred and forty.

SECOND SENATOR

And mine say two hundred. But often in these cases, reports are just estimates. The important thing is that they all say a Turkish fleet is approaching Cyprus.

DUKE

Yes, we get the idea. The inconsistency doesn't make me think that the reports are all wrong. I have no doubt about what they're basically saying, and it's frightening.

SAILOR

(offstage) Hello! Hey, hello!

OFFICER

It's a messenger from the warships.

A SAILOR *enters.*

DUKE

Why are you here?

SAILOR

Signor Angelo told me to come here and tell you that the Turkish fleet is heading for Rhodes, not Cyprus.

DUKE
How say you by this change?

FIRST SENATOR
                                            This cannot be,
20   By no assay of reason. 'Tis a pageant,
        To keep us in false gaze. When we consider
        Th' importancy of Cyprus to the Turk,
        And let ourselves again but understand
        That as it more concerns the Turk than Rhodes
25   So may he with more facile question bear it,
        For that it stands not in such warlike brace
        But altogether lacks th' abilities
        That Rhodes is dressed in. If we make thought of this
        We must not think the Turk is so unskillful
30   To leave that latest which concerns him first,
        Neglecting an attempt of ease and gain
        To wake and wage a danger profitless.

DUKE
Nay, in all confidence, he's not for Rhodes.

OFFICER
Here is more news.

Enter a MESSENGER

MESSENGER
35   The Ottomites, reverend and gracious,
        Steering with due course toward the isle of Rhodes,
        Have there injointed them with an after fleet.

FIRST SENATOR
Ay, so I thought. How many, as you guess?

MESSENGER
        Of thirty sail. And now they do re-stem
40   Their backward course, bearing with frank appearance
        Their purposes toward Cyprus. Signior Montano,
        Your trusty and most valiant servitor,
        With his free duty recommends you thus,
        And prays you to believe him.

DUKE

What do you think about this change?

FIRST SENATOR

They can't have changed; there's no way this could be true. It's a trick to confuse us. Think about how important Cyprus is to the Turks, and remember that they could capture Cyprus more easily, since it isn't as well protected as Rhodes is. If we keep these things in mind, we can't possibly imagine that the Turks would be so incompetent as to put off for last what they want to achieve first, setting aside something easy and profitable to do something dangerous and pointless.

DUKE

No, I think we can be confident that the Turks aren't really headed for Rhodes.

OFFICER

Here's some more news coming in.

A MESSENGER enters.

MESSENGER

Sir, the Turks sailed to Rhodes, where they joined with another fleet.

FIRST SENATOR

That's just what I thought. How many, can you guess?

MESSENGER

Thirty ships. Now they've turned around and are clearly heading for Cyprus. Signor Montano, your brave and loyal servant, gives you this information and asks you to send reinforcements to relieve him.

DUKE

'Tis certain then for Cyprus.

45   Marcus Luccicos, is not he in town?

FIRST SENATOR

He's now in Florence.

DUKE

Write from us to him. Post-post-haste, dispatch.

FIRST SENATOR

Here comes Brabantio and the valiant Moor.

Enter BRABANTIO, OTHELLO, CASSIO, IAGO, RODERIGO, *and officers*

DUKE

Valiant Othello, we must straight employ you

50   Against the general enemy Ottoman—

(to BRABANTIO*)* I did not see you. Welcome, gentle signior.

We lacked your counsel and your help tonight.

BRABANTIO

So did I yours. Good your grace, pardon me.

Neither my place nor aught I heard of business

55   Hath raised me from my bed, nor doth the general care

Take hold on me, for my particular grief

Is of so flood-gate and o'erbearing nature

That it engluts and swallows other sorrows

And it is still itself.

DUKE

60   Why, what's the matter?

BRABANTIO

My daughter! Oh, my daughter!

ALL

Dead?

BRABANTIO

Ay, to me.

She is abused, stol'n from me, and corrupted

By spells and medicines bought of mountebanks.

DUKE

Then it's certain they're heading for Cyprus. Is Marcus Luccicos in town?

FIRST SENATOR

No, he's in Florence.

DUKE

Write to him immediately. Hurry.

FIRST SENATOR

Here come Brabantio and the brave Moor.

BRABANTIO, OTHELLO, CASSIO, IAGO, RODERIGO *and the officers enter.*

DUKE

Brave Othello, I have to send you right away to fight the Turks, our great enemy.—*(to* BRABANTIO*)* Oh, I didn't see you there. Welcome, sir. I could have used your wisdom and help tonight.

BRABANTIO

I could have used yours as well. Forgive me, your grace. I didn't get out of bed and come here in the dead of night because I heard about the war or because I was worried about the city's defense. I have a personal problem so painful and gut-wrenching that it overwhelms everything else.

DUKE

Why, what's the matter?

BRABANTIO

It's my daughter! Oh, my daughter!

FIRST SENATOR

Is she dead?

BRABANTIO

She's dead to me. She's been tricked and stolen from me, enchanted by black magic spells. She must've

For nature so prepost'rously to err,
65   Being not deficient, blind, or lame of sense,
Sans witchcraft could not.

DUKE
Whoe'er he be that in this foul proceeding
Hath thus beguiled your daughter of herself
And you of her, the bloody book of law
70   You shall yourself read in the bitter letter,
After your own sense, yea, though our proper son
Stood in your action.

BRABANTIO
                Humbly I thank your grace.
Here is the man, this Moor, whom now it seems,
Your special mandate for the state affairs
75   Hath hither brought.

ALL
                We are very sorry for't.

DUKE
(to OTHELLO*)* What, in your own part, can you say to this?

BRABANTIO
Nothing, but this is so.

OTHELLO
Most potent, grave, and reverend signiors,
My very noble and approved good masters,
80   That I have ta'en away this old man's daughter,
It is most true. True, I have married her.
The very head and front of my offending
Hath this extent, no more. Rude am I in my speech,
And little blessed with the soft phrase of peace,
85   For since these arms of mine had seven years' pith
Till now some nine moons wasted, they have used
Their dearest action in the tented field,
And little of this great world can I speak,

been tricked or drugged, because there's no way she could have made this mistake on her own.

DUKE

Whoever tricked your daughter and stole her from you will pay for it. And you yourself will determine the sentence as you see fit, and impose the death penalty if you choose to, even if the criminal were my own son.

BRABANTIO

I humbly thank you, sir. Here is the man, the Moor. It seems you had your own reasons for summoning him here.

ALL

We're sorry to hear this.

DUKE

(to OTHELLO*)* What do you have to say for yourself?

BRABANTIO

Nothing, but this is true.

OTHELLO

Noble, honorable gentlemen whom I serve: it's true that I've taken this man's daughter from him and married her. But that's my only offense. There's nothing more. I'm awkward in my speech and I'm not a smooth talker. From the time I was seven years old until nine months ago I've been fighting in battles. I don't know much about the world apart from fighting. So I won't do myself much good by speaking in my own defense. But if you'll let me, I'll tell you the plain

More than pertains to feats of broils and battle,
90   And therefore little shall I grace my cause
In speaking for myself. Yet, by your gracious patience,
I will a round unvarnished tale deliver
Of my whole course of love. What drugs, what charms,
What conjuration and what mighty magic—
95   For such proceeding I am charged withal—
I won his daughter.

BRABANTIO
                                    A maiden never bold,
Of spirit so still and quiet that her motion
Blushed at herself. And she, in spite of nature,
Of years, of country, credit, everything,
100   To fall in love with what she feared to look on?
It is a judgment maimed and most imperfect
That will confess perfection so could err.
Against all rules of nature, and must be driven
To find out practices of cunning hell
105   Why this should be. I therefore vouch again
That with some mixtures powerful o'er the blood
Or with some dram, conjured to this effect,
He wrought upon her.

DUKE
                                    To vouch this is no proof,
Without more wider and more overt test
110   Than these thin habits and poor likelihoods
Of modern seeming do prefer against him.

FIRST SENATOR
But, Othello, speak.
Did you by indirect and forcèd courses
Subdue and poison this young maid's affections?
115   Or came it by request and such fair question
As soul to soul affordeth?

OTHELLO
                                    I do beseech you,
Send for the lady to the Sagittary,

story of how we fell in love, and what drugs, charms, spells, and powerful magic—because that's what I'm being accused of—I used to win his daughter.

BRABANTIO

She's a good girl, quiet and obedient. She blushes at the slightest thing. And you want me to believe that despite her young age and proper upbringing she fell in love with a man she'd be afraid to look at? The very thought of it is ridiculous. You'd have to be stupid to think that someone so perfect could make such an unnatural mistake as that. The devil must be behind this. Therefore I say again that he must have used some powerful drug or magic potion on her.

DUKE

you're

Your saying this isn't proof. There has to be clear evidence that he's done this, not just these accusations.

FIRST SENATOR

Tell us, Othello. Did you trick or deceive this lady in some way? Or did you agree to this as equals?

OTHELLO

Please, send for Desdemona to come here from the Sagittarius Inn and ask her to speak about me in front

And let her speak of me before her father.
If you do find me foul in her report
120   The trust, the office I do hold of you,
Not only take away, but let your sentence
Even fall upon my life.

DUKE

Fetch Desdemona hither.

OTHELLO

Ancient, conduct them. You best know the place.

Exeunt IAGO *and attendants*

And till she come, as truly as to heaven
125   I do confess the vices of my blood
So justly to your grave ears I'll present
How I did thrive in this fair lady's love
And she in mine.

DUKE

Say it, Othello.

OTHELLO

Her father loved me, oft invited me,
130   Still questioned me the story of my life
From year to year, the battles, sieges, fortunes,
That I have passed.
I ran it through, even from my boyish days,
To th' very moment that he bade me tell it,
135   Wherein I spoke of most disastrous chances,
Of moving accidents by flood and field,
Of hair-breadth 'scapes i' th' imminent deadly breach,
Of being taken by the insolent foe
And sold to slavery, of my redemption thence
140   And portance in my traveler's history.
Wherein of antres vast and deserts idle,
Rough quarries, rocks, hills whose heads touch heaven
It was my hint to speak—such was my process—
And of the Cannibals that each others eat,

of her father. If she has anything bad to say about me, then you can sentence me to death.

DUKE

Bring Desdemona here.

OTHELLO

Iago, bring Desdemona here. You know where she is.

IAGO and attendants exit.

In the meantime I'll tell you all, as honestly as I confess my sins to God, how I wooed this beautiful lady, and how she came to love me.

DUKE

Tell us, Othello.

OTHELLO

Her father loved me and used to invite me to his house often, continually asking me about my life and all the battles I've fought. I told him everything, from my boyhood up until the time when I was talking to him. I told him about unfortunate disasters, hair-raising adventures on sea and on land, and near-catastrophes and dangerous adventures I've been through. I told him how I was captured and sold as a slave, how I bought my freedom, and how I wandered through caves and deserts. I was able to tell him about cannibals who eat each other, and men with heads growing below their shoulders. When I talked about all these things, Desdemona used to listen attentively. If she had to go do some household chore, I noticed that she'd always come back quickly to hear more of my stories.

145   The Anthropophagi, and men whose heads
Grew beneath their shoulders. These things to hear
Would Desdemona seriously incline.
But still the house affairs would draw her hence,
Which ever as she could with haste dispatch,
150   She'd come again, and with a greedy ear
Devour up my discourse, which I, observing,
Took once a pliant hour and found good means
To draw from her a prayer of earnest heart
That I would all my pilgrimage dilate,
155   Whereof by parcels she had something heard
But not intentively. I did consent,
And often did beguile her of her tears
When I did speak of some distressful stroke
That my youth suffered. My story being done
160   She gave me for my pains a world of sighs.
She swore, in faith, 'twas strange, 'twas passing strange,
'Twas pitiful, 'twas wondrous pitiful.
She wished she had not heard it, yet she wished
That heaven had made her such a man. She thanked me
165   And bade me, if I had a friend that loved her,
I should but teach him how to tell my story
And that would woo her. Upon this hint I spake.
She loved me for the dangers I had passed,
And I loved her that she did pity them.
170   This only is the witchcraft I have used.
Here comes the lady. Let her witness it.

Enter DESDEMONA, IAGO, *and attendants*

DUKE
    I think this tale would win my daughter too.
Good Brabantio. Take up this mangled matter at the best.
Men do their broken weapons rather use
175   Than their bare hands.

When I was relaxing, she'd pull me aside and ask to hear some part of a story she had missed. Her eyes would fill with tears at the bad things I went through in my younger years. When my stories were done, she'd sigh and tell me how strangely wonderful and sad my life had been. She said she wished she hadn't heard it, but she also wished there was a man like me for her. She thanked me and told me that if a friend of mine had a story like mine to tell, she'd fall in love with him. I took the hint and spoke to her. She said she loved me for the dangers I'd survived, and I loved her for feeling such strong emotions about me. That's the only witchcraft I ever used. Here comes my wife now. She'll confirm everything.

DESDEMONA, IAGO, *and attendants enter.*

DUKE

I think a story like that would win my own daughter over. Brabantio, I urge you to make the best of this. Try to accept what's happened.

BRABANTIO

                              I pray you, hear her speak.
If she confess that she was half the wooer,
Destruction on my head if my bad blame
Light on the man.—Come hither, gentle mistress.
Do you perceive in all this noble company
180   Where most you owe obedience?

DESDEMONA

                               My noble father,
I do perceive here a divided duty.
To you I am bound for life and education.
My life and education both do learn me
How to respect you. You are the lord of duty.
185   I am hitherto your daughter. But here's my husband.
And so much duty as my mother showed
To you, preferring you before her father,
So much I challenge that I may profess
Due to the Moor my lord.

BRABANTIO

                        God be with you. I have done.
190   Please it your grace, on to the state affairs.
I had rather to adopt a child than get it.—
Come hither, Moor.
I here do give thee that with all my heart
Which, but thou hast already, with all my heart
195   I would keep from thee. For your sake, jewel,
I am glad at soul I have no other child.
For thy escape would teach me tyranny,
To hang clogs on them.—I have done, my lord.

DUKE

Let me speak like yourself and lay a sentence
200   Which, as a grise or step, may help these lovers.
When remedies are past, the griefs are ended
By seeing the worst, which late on hopes depended.

BRABANTIO

Please let her speak. If she admits she wanted this, then I won't blame Othello.—Come here, my child. Who do you obey here?

DESDEMONA

Father, this isn't easy for me. I'm torn. I owe you respect because you gave me life and education. You're the one I have to obey. I'm your daughter. But this man here is my husband now, and I owe him as much as my mother owed you, just as she preferred you to her own father. So I have to give my obedience to the Moor, my husband.

BRABANTIO

I'm finished, then. Duke, please go ahead with your state business. I'd rather adopt a child than have one of my own.—Come here, Moor. I'm forced to give my blessing to this marriage. With all my heart, I give you that thing which, if you didn't already have it, I'd try with all my heart to keep from you. Desdemona, I'm glad you're my only child, since if I had others I'd keep them all locked up. You would have made me treat them like a tyrant.—I'm done, my lord.

DUKE

Let me refer to a proverb that may help you forgive these lovers: if you can't change something, don't cry about it. When you lament something bad that's already happened, you're setting yourself up for more

To mourn a mischief that is past and gone
Is the next way to draw new mischief on.
205 What cannot be preserved when fortune takes,
Patience her injury a mock'ry makes.
The robbed that smiles steals something from the thief,
He robs himself that spends a bootless grief.

BRABANTIO
So let the Turk of Cyprus us beguile,
210 We lose it not, so long as we can smile.
He bears the sentence well that nothing bears
But the free comfort which from thence he hears.
But he bears both the sentence and the sorrow
That, to pay grief, must of poor patience borrow.
215 These sentences to sugar or to gall,
Being strong on both sides, are equivocal.
But words are words. I never yet did hear
That the bruisèd heart was piercèd through the ears.
I humbly beseech you, proceed to th' affairs of state.

DUKE
220 The Turk with a most mighty preparation makes for
Cyprus. Othello, the fortitude of the place is best known
to you, and though we have there a substitute of most
allowed sufficiency, yet opinion, a sovereign mistress of
effects, throws a more safer voice on you. You must therefore
225 be content to slubber the gloss of your new fortunes with
this more stubborn and boist'rous expedition.

OTHELLO
The tyrant custom, most grave senators,
Hath made the flinty and steel couch of war
My thrice-driven bed of down. I do agnize
230 A natural and prompt alacrity
I find in hardness, and do undertake
These present wars against the Ottomites.
Most humbly therefore bending to your state,

bad news. A robbery victim who can smile about his losses is superior to the thief who robbed him, but if he cries he's just wasting time.

BRABANTIO

So if the Turks steal Cyprus from us, it won't be bad as long as we keep smiling. It's easy to accept platitudes like that if you haven't lost anything. But I've lost something precious, and I have to put up with the platitude as well as suffering my loss. Talk is cheap. I've never heard of someone feeling better because of someone else's words. Please, I'm asking you, go ahead and get back to your state affairs.

DUKE

The Turks are heading for Cyprus with a powerful fleet. Othello, you understand better than anyone how the defenses for Cyprus work. Even though we have a very good officer in charge there already, everyone says you're the better man for the job. So I'll have to ask you to put a damper on your marriage celebrations and take part in this dangerous expedition.

OTHELLO

I've gotten used to the hardships of a military life. I rise to the occasion when faced with difficulties. I will take charge of this war against the Turks. But I humbly ask you to make appropriate arrangements for my

        I crave fit disposition for my wife.

235   Due reference of place and exhibition,

        With such accommodation and besort

        As levels with her breeding.

DUKE

        Why, at her father's.

BRABANTIO

        I'll not have it so.

OTHELLO

240   Nor I.

DESDEMONA

        Nor would I there reside,

        To put my father in impatient thoughts

        By being in his eye. Most gracious Duke,

        To my unfolding lend your prosperous ear

245   And let me find a charter in your voice,

        T' assist my simpleness.

DUKE

        What would you, Desdemona?

DESDEMONA

        That I did love the Moor to live with him,

        My downright violence and storm of fortunes

250   May trumpet to the world. My heart's subdued

        Even to the very quality of my lord.

        I saw Othello's visage in his mind,

        And to his honors and his valiant parts

        Did I my soul and fortunes consecrate.

255   So that, dear lords, if I be left behind

        A moth of peace and he go to the war,

        The rites for which I love him are bereft me,

        And I a heavy interim shall support

        By his dear absence. Let me go with him.

OTHELLO

260   Let her have your voice.

        Vouch with me, heaven, I therefore beg it not

        To please the palate of my appetite,

wife, giving her a place to live and people to keep her company that suit her high rank.

DUKE

She can stay at her father's house.

BRABANTIO

I won't allow it.

OTHELLO

Neither will I.

DESDEMONA

And I wouldn't stay there. I don't want to upset my father by being in his house. Dear Duke, please listen to what I have to say.

DUKE

What do you want to do, Desdemona?

DESDEMONA

When I fell in love with Othello I made up my mind that I wanted to live with him. You can see how much I wanted to be with him by how violently I threw away my old life. I feel like I'm a part of him now, and that means I'm part of a soldier. I saw Othello's true face when I saw his mind. I gave my whole life to him because of his honor and bravery. If I were left at home uselessly while he went off to war, then I'm separated from my husband in his natural element. I'd be miserable without him. Let me go with him.

OTHELLO

Please allow her to do this. I'm not asking to have her near me for sex—I'm too old for that, and my sexual

Nor to comply with heat the young affects
In my defunct and proper satisfaction,
265   But to be free and bounteous to her mind,
And heaven defend your good souls, that you think
I will your serious and great business scant
When she is with me. No, when light-winged toys
Of feathered Cupid seel with wanton dullness
270   My speculative and officed instrument,
That my disports corrupt and taint my business,
Let housewives make a skillet of my helm
And all indign and base adversities
Make head against my estimation.

DUKE
275   Be it as you shall privately determine,
Either for her stay or going. Th' affair cries haste
And speed must answer it.

FIRST SENATOR
                                                    You must away tonight.

OTHELLO
With all my heart.

DUKE
At nine i' th' morning here we'll meet again.
280   Othello, leave some officer behind
And he shall our commission bring to you,
And such things else of quality and respect
As doth import you.

OTHELLO
                                    So please your grace, my ancient.
A man he is of honesty and trust.
285   To his conveyance I assign my wife,
With what else needful your good grace shall think
To be sent after me.

urges are dead. I want this because she wants it—I love her for her mind. And I'd never want you to think that I'd neglect my serious official duties while she was there with me. If I ever let love blind me so that I choose to lounge around in bed with my loved one instead of going off to war, then you can let a housewife use my helmet as a frying pan. My reputation would be disgraced if I ever acted like that.

DUKE

You can decide that privately. I don't care whether she stays or goes. What's important is the urgency of this mission. You've got to act fast.

FIRST SENATOR

You'll have to leave tonight.

OTHELLO

With all my heart, I'll go right away.

DUKE

We'll meet again at nine in the morning. Othello, have one of your officers stay behind to bring you your commission and whatever else is important to you.

OTHELLO

My lord, my ensign is an honest and trustworthy man. He'll accompany my wife, and bring whatever else you think I might need.

DUKE
> Let it be so.
> Good night to every one.—*(to* BRABANTIO*)*
> And, noble signior,
290   If virtue no delighted beauty lack,
> Your son-in-law is far more fair than black.

FIRST SENATOR
> Adieu, brave Moor. Use Desdemona well.

BRABANTIO
> Look to her, Moor, if thou hast eyes to see.
> She has deceived her father, and may thee.

> *Exeunt* DUKE, BRABANTIO, CASSIO, SENATORS, *and*
> *officers*

OTHELLO
295   My life upon her faith!—Honest Iago,
> My Desdemona must I leave to thee.
> I prithee, let thy wife attend on her,
> And bring them after in the best advantage.
> Come, Desdemona, I have but an hour
300   Of love, of worldly matter and direction,
> To spend with thee. We must obey the time.

> *Exeunt* OTHELLO *and* DESDEMONA

RODERIGO
> Iago.

IAGO
> What say'st thou, noble heart?

RODERIGO
> What will I do, think'st thou?

IAGO
305   Why, go to bed, and sleep.

RODERIGO
> I will incontinently drown myself.

DUKE

All right, then. Good night, everyone.—*(to* BRABAN-TIO*)* Sir, if goodness is beautiful, your son-in-law is beautiful, not black.

FIRST SENATOR

Goodbye, black Moor. Treat Desdemona well.

BRABANTIO

Keep an eye on her, Moor. She lied to me, and she may lie to you.

The DUKE, BRABANTIO, CASSIO, SENATORS, *and officers exit.*

OTHELLO

I'd bet my life she'd never lie to me. Iago, I'm leaving my dear Desdemona with you. Have your wife attend to her, and bring them along as soon as you can. Come on, Desdemona, I've only got an hour of love to spend with you, to tell you what you need to do. We're on a tight schedule.

OTHELLO *and* DESDEMONA *exit.*

RODERIGO

Iago.

IAGO

What do you have to say, noble friend?

RODERIGO

What do you think I should do?

IAGO

Go to bed, and sleep.

RODERIGO

I'm going to go drown myself.

IAGO

If thou dost I shall never love thee after. Why, thou silly
gentleman!

RODERIGO

It is silliness to live when to live is torment, and then have
310   we a prescription to die when death is our physician.

IAGO

Oh, villainous! I have looked upon the world for four
times seven years, and since I could distinguish betwixt a
benefit and an injury I never found man that knew how to
love himself. Ere I would say I would drown myself for the
315   love of a guinea hen, I would change my humanity with a
baboon.

RODERIGO

What should I do? I confess it is my shame to be so fond,
but it is not in my virtue to amend it.

IAGO

Virtue? A fig! 'Tis in ourselves that we are thus or thus.
320   Our bodies are our gardens, to the which our wills are
gardeners. So that if we will plant nettles or sow lettuce,
set hyssop and weed up thyme, supply it with one gender
of herbs or distract it with many—either to have it sterile
with idleness, or manured with industry—why, the power
325   and corrigible authority of this lies in our wills. If the
balance of our lives had not one scale of reason to poise
another of sensuality, the blood and baseness of our
natures would conduct us to most prepost'rous
conclusions. But we have reason to cool our raging
330   motions, our carnal stings, our unbitted lusts. Whereof I
take this that you call love to be a sect or scion.

RODERIGO

It cannot be.

IAGO

It is merely a lust of the blood and a permission of the will.
Come, be a man. Drown thyself? Drown cats and blind
335.   puppies! I have professed me thy friend, and I confess me

IAGO

If you do that, I'll never respect you again. Why, you silly man!

RODERIGO

It's silly to live when life is torture. The only cure is death.

IAGO

Oh, how stupid! I've been alive for twenty-eight years, and I've never met a man who knew what was good for him. I'd rather be a baboon than kill myself out of love for some woman I can't have.

RODERIGO

What should I do? I know it's foolish to be so much in love, but I can't help it.

IAGO

Can't help it? Nonsense! What we are is up to us. Our bodies are like gardens and our willpower is like the gardener. Depending on what we plant—weeds or lettuce, or one kind of herb rather than a variety, the garden will either be barren and useless, or rich and productive. If we didn't have rational minds to counterbalance our emotions and desires, our bodily urges would take over. We'd end up in ridiculous situations. Thankfully, we have reason to cool our raging lusts. In my opinion, what you call love is just an offshoot of lust.

RODERIGO

I don't believe it.

IAGO

You feel love because you feel lust and you have no willpower. Come on, be a man. Drown yourself? Drowning is for cats or blind puppies—don't drown yourself! I've told you I'm your friend, and I'll stick by

knit to thy deserving with cables of perdurable toughness.
I could never better stead thee than now. Put money in thy
purse. Follow thou the wars, defeat thy favor with an
usurped beard. I say, put money in thy purse. It cannot be
340 long that Desdemona should continue her love to the
Moor—put money in thy purse—nor he his to her. It was
a violent commencement in her, and thou shalt see an
answerable sequestration—put but money in thy purse.
These Moors are changeable in their wills—fill thy purse
345 with money. The food that to him now is as luscious as
locusts shall be to him shortly as bitter as coloquintida.
She must change for youth. When she is sated with his
body she will find the errors of her choice. Therefore, put
money in thy purse. If thou wilt needs damn thyself, do it
350 a more delicate way than drowning. Make all the money
thou canst. If sanctimony and a frail vow betwixt an erring
barbarian and supersubtle Venetian be not too hard for my
wits and all the tribe of hell, thou shalt enjoy her.
Therefore make money. A pox of drowning thyself! 'Tis
355 clean out of the way. Seek thou rather to be hanged in
compassing thy joy than to be drowned and go without her.

RODERIGO

Wilt thou be fast to my hopes, if I depend on the issue?

IAGO

Thou art sure of me. Go, make money. I have told thee
often, and I re-tell thee again and again, I hate the Moor.
360 My cause is hearted. Thine hath no less reason. Let us be
conjunctive in our revenge against him. If thou canst
cuckold him, thou dost thyself a pleasure, me a sport.
There are many events in the womb of time which will be
delivered. Traverse, go, provide thy money. We will have
365 more of this tomorrow. Adieu.

RODERIGO

Where shall we meet i' th' morning?

you. I've never been more useful to you than I will be now. Here's what you'll do. Sell all your assets and your land, and turn it into cash. Desdemona can't continue loving the Moor any more than he can continue loving her. She fell in love with him very suddenly, and they'll break up just as suddenly. Moors are moody people.—So sell your lands and raise a lot of cash. What seems sweet to him now will soon turn bitter. She'll dump Othello for a younger man. When she's had enough of the Moor's body, she'll realize her mistake. She'll need to have a new lover. She'll have to have it. So have your money ready. If you want to go to hell, there are better ways to do it than killing yourself. Raise all the money you can. I can get the better of religion and a few flimsy vows between a misguided barbarian and a depraved Venetian girl. You'll get to sleep with her—just put together some money. And to hell with drowning yourself! That's completely beside the point. If you're ready to die, you can risk death by committing crimes in an attempt to get the woman you want. Don't just give up on her and drown yourself.

RODERIGO

Can I count on you if I wait to see what happens?

IAGO

You can trust me. Go now and get cash. I told you before, and I'll tell you again and again: I hate the Moor. I'm devoted to my cause of hating him, just as devoted as you are to yours. So let's join forces and get revenge. If you seduce Desdemona and make a fool out of him, it'll be fun for both of us. Many things may happen. Go get money. We'll speak again tomorrow. Goodbye.

RODERIGO

Where will we meet in the morning?

IAGO

                                                        At my lodging.

RODERIGO
        I'll be with thee betimes.

IAGO

                                        Go to, farewell.
        Do you hear, Roderigo?

RODERIGO
        What say you?

IAGO
370   No more of drowning, do you hear?

RODERIGO
        I am changed.

IAGO
        Go to, farewell. Put money enough in your purse.

RODERIGO
        I'll sell all my land.

                                                        Exit

IAGO
        Thus do I ever make my fool my purse.
375   For I mine own gained knowledge should profane
        If I would time expend with such a snipe
        But for my sport and profit. I hate the Moor,
        And it is thought abroad that 'twixt my sheets
        He's done my office. I know not if 't be true,
380   But I, for mere suspicion in that kind,
        Will do as if for surety. He holds me well.
        The better shall my purpose work on him.
        Cassio's a proper man. Let me see now,

IAGO

At my house.

RODERIGO

I'll be there early.

IAGO

Go home. Goodbye. Oh, and one more thing—

RODERIGO

What is it?

IAGO

No more talk about killing yourself, okay?

RODERIGO

I've changed my mind about that.

IAGO

Go then, goodbye. Put a lot of cash together.

RODERIGO

I'm going to sell all my land.

RODERIGO exits.

IAGO

That's how I always do it, getting money from fools.
I'd be wasting my skills dealing with an idiot like that
if I couldn't get something useful out of him. I hate the
Moor, and there's a widespread rumor that he's slept
with my wife. I'm not sure it's true, but just the suspicion is enough for me. He thinks highly of me.
That'll help. Cassio's a handsome man. Let's see, how

To get his place and to plume up my will
385 In double knavery. How? How? Let's see.
After some time, to abuse Othello's ear
That he is too familiar with his wife.
He hath a person and a smooth dispose
To be suspected, framed to make women false.
390 The Moor is of a free and open nature
That thinks men honest that but seem to be so,
And will as tenderly be led by th' nose
As asses are.
I have 't. It is engendered! Hell and night
395 Must bring this monstrous birth to the world's light.

Exit

can I get his position and use him to hurt Othello at the same time? How? How? Let's see. After a while I'll start telling Othello that Cassio is too intimate with Desdemona. Cassio is a smooth talker and a good-looking guy, the sort of man that people would expect to be a seducer. The Moor is open and straightforward. He thinks any man who seems honest is honest. People like that are easy to manipulate. So it's all decided. I've worked it out. With a little help from the devil, I'll bring this monstrous plan to success.

He exits.

ACT TWO

SCENE 1

Enter MONTANO *and two* GENTLEMEN

MONTANO
What from the cape can you discern at sea?

FIRST GENTLEMAN
Nothing at all. It is a high-wrought flood.
I cannot 'twixt the heaven and the main
5   Descry a sail.

MONTANO
Methinks the wind hath spoke aloud at land,
A fuller blast ne'er shook our battlements.
If it hath ruffianed so upon the sea
What ribs of oak, when mountains melt on them,
10   Can hold the mortise? What shall we hear of this?

SECOND GENTLEMAN
A segregation of the Turkish fleet.
For do but stand upon the foaming shore,
The chidden billow seems to pelt the clouds,
The wind-shaked surge, with high and monstrous mane,
15   Seems to cast water on the burning bear,
And quench the guards of th' ever-fixèd pole.
I never did like molestation view
On the enchafèd flood.

MONTANO
If that the Turkish fleet
20   Be not ensheltered and embayed, they are drowned.
It is impossible they bear it out.

Enter a THIRD GENTLEMAN

ACT TWO
SCENE 1

MONTANO *and two* GENTLEMEN *enter.*

MONTANO
> What can you see out on the ocean?

FIRST GENTLEMAN
> Nothing. The water's so rough that I can't see any sails, either in the bay or on the ocean.

MONTANO
> It was windy on shore too. A big blast of wind shook our fortifications. How could a ship made out of wood hold together in those mountainous waves? What do you think will be the result of this storm?

SECOND GENTLEMAN
> The Turkish navy will be broken up. The wind's whipping up the waves so high you expect them to reach the clouds and splash against the stars in the sky. I've never seen the waters so disturbed.

MONTANO
> If the Turkish fleet isn't protected in some harbor, their men must all be drowned. No ship could survive this storm.

A THIRD GENTLEMAN *enters.*

THIRD GENTLEMAN
News, lads, Our wars are done!
The desperate tempest hath so banged the Turks,
That their designment halts. A noble ship of Venice
25   Hath seen a grievous wreck and sufferance
On most part of their fleet.

MONTANO
How? Is this true?

THIRD GENTLEMAN
                    The ship is here put in,
A Veronesa. Michael Cassio,
Lieutenant to the warlike Moor Othello,
30   Is come on shore. The Moor himself at sea
And is in full commission here for Cyprus.

MONTANO
I am glad on 't. 'Tis a worthy governor.

THIRD GENTLEMAN
But this same Cassio, though he speak of comfort
Touching the Turkish loss, yet he looks sadly
35   And prays the Moor be safe. For they were parted
With foul and violent tempest.

MONTANO
                    Pray heavens he be,
For I have served him, and the man commands
Like a full soldier. Let's to the seaside, ho!
As well to see the vessel that's come in
40   As to throw out our eyes for brave Othello,
Even till we make the main and th' aerial blue
An indistinct regard.

THIRD GENTLEMAN
                Come, let's do so.
For every minute is expectancy
Of more arrivance.

Enter CASSIO

THIRD GENTLEMAN

I've got news, boys, the war's over! This terrible storm has smashed the Turks so badly that their plans are ruined. One of our ships has reported that it saw most of their fleet shipwrecked.

MONTANO

What? Is this true?

THIRD GENTLEMAN

The ship's sailing into harbor now; it's from Verona. Michael Cassio, lieutenant of the Moor Othello, has arrived on shore. The Moor himself is still at sea. He's been commissioned to come here to Cyprus.

MONTANO

I'm happy about that. He'll be a good governor.

THIRD GENTLEMAN

Cassio brings good news about the Turkish defeat, but he's worried about the Othello's safety. The two of them were separated during the storm.

MONTANO

I hope to God Othello's all right. I served under him, and I know what an excellent commander he is. Let's go to the shore to get a look at the ship that came in, and to look out for Othello's ship. We'll stare out at the sea until the sea and the sky blur together.

THIRD GENTLEMAN

Let's do that. Every minute we expect more ships to arrive.

CASSIO *enters.*

CASSIO

45   Thanks, you the valiant of this warlike isle
        That so approve the Moor. Oh, let the heavens
        Give him defense against the elements,
        For I have lost him on a dangerous sea.

MONTANO

        Is he well shipped?

CASSIO

50   His bark is stoutly timbered and his pilot
        Of very expert and approved allowance
        Therefore my hopes, not surfeited to death,
        Stand in bold cure.

A VOICE

        (within) A sail, a sail, a sail!

Enter a MESSENGER

CASSIO

55   What noise?

MESSENGER

        The town is empty. On the brow o' th' sea
        Stand ranks of people, and they cry "A sail!"

CASSIO

        My hopes do shape him for the governor.

A shot

SECOND GENTLEMAN

        They do discharge their shot of courtesy.
60   Our friends at least.

CASSIO

        I pray you sir, go forth
        And give us truth who 'tis that is arrived.

SECOND GENTLEMAN

        I shall.

Exit

CASSIO

Thanks, you brave men who defend this island and respect Othello. I hope heaven protects him from the weather, because I lost sight of him on the stormy sea.

MONTANO

Is his ship sturdy?

CASSIO

Yes, it's well built, and the ship's pilot is very expert and experienced. For that reason I still have some hope for him, even though I don't have my hopes up too high.

A VOICE

(offstage) A sail! A sail! A sail!

A MESSENGER enters.

CASSIO

What's all that shouting about?

MESSENGER

Everybody in town is down at the shore shouting "A sail!"

CASSIO

I hope it's Othello.

A shot is heard.

SECOND GENTLEMAN

They've fired a greeting shot, so at least it's a friendly ship.

CASSIO

Please go find out for certain who has arrived.

SECOND GENTLEMAN

I'll do that.

SECOND GENTLEMAN exits.

MONTANO
But good lieutenant, is your general wived?

CASSIO
65 Most fortunately. He hath achieved a maid
That paragons description and wild fame,
One that excels the quirks of blazoning pens,
And in th' essential vesture of creation
Does tire the ingener.

Enter SECOND GENTLEMAN

70 How now? Who has put in?

SECOND GENTLEMAN
'Tis one Iago, ancient to the general.

CASSIO
He's had most favorable and happy speed.
Tempests themselves, high seas, and howling winds,
The guttered rocks and congregated sands,
75 Traitors ensteeped to enclog the guiltless keel,
As having sense of beauty, do omit
Their mortal natures, letting go safely by
The divine Desdemona.

MONTANO
What is she?

CASSIO
80 She that I spake of, our great captain's captain,
Left in the conduct of the bold Iago,
Whose footing here anticipates our thoughts
A se'nnight's speed. Great Jove, Othello guard,
And swell his sail with thine own powerful breath,
85 That he may bless this bay with his tall ship,
Make love's quick pants in Desdemona's arms,
Give renewed fire to our extinct spirits
And bring all Cyprus comfort!

MONTANO

Good lieutenant, is your general married?

CASSIO

Yes, and he's very lucky to have married the woman he did. His wife defies description. She's God's masterpiece, and she'd exhaust whoever tried to do her justice while praising her.

The SECOND GENTLEMAN *enters.*

Who's arrived in the harbor?

SECOND GENTLEMAN

A man named Iago, the general's ensign.

CASSIO

He made good time. You see how the storm, the jagged rocks, and the sand banks that trap ships all appreciate a beautiful woman. They let the heavenly Desdemona arrive safe and sound.

MONTANO

Who's that?

CASSIO

She's the one I was talking about, the general's wife. The brave Iago was put in charge of bringing her here, and he's arrived a week sooner than we expected. Dear God, please protect Othello and help him arrive here safely, so he and Desdemona can be in each other's arms, and Othello can cheer us up and bring comfort to Cyprus.

Enter DESDEMONA, EMILIA, IAGO, RODERIGO *with attendants*

                                    Oh, behold,
The riches of the ship is come on shore!
90   You men of Cyprus, let her have your knees.
Hail to thee, lady, and the grace of heaven,
Before, behind thee, and on every hand,
Enwheel thee round!

DESDEMONA
I thank you, valiant Cassio.
95   What tidings can you tell me of my lord?

CASSIO
He is not yet arrived. Nor know I aught
But that he's well and will be shortly here.

DESDEMONA
Oh, but I fear. How lost you company?

CASSIO
The great contention of the sea and skies
100   Parted our fellowship—

A VOICE
(within) A sail, a sail!

CASSIO
But, hark! a sail.

A shot

SECOND GENTLEMAN
They give this greeting to the citadel.
This likewise is a friend.

CASSIO
                                    See for the news.

Exit a SECOND GENTLEMEN

DESDEMONA, IAGO, RODERIGO *and* EMILIA *enter.*

Look, the precious Desdemona has arrived on shore. We should all kneel before her, men of Cyprus! Greetings, my lady, and may God always be with you.

DESDEMONA

Thank you, brave Cassio. Is there any news about my husband?

CASSIO

He hasn't arrived yet. As far as I know, he's okay and will arrive here soon.

DESDEMONA

Oh, but I'm worried. How did you two get separated?

CASSIO

The storm separated us.

A VOICE

(offstage) A sail! A sail!

CASSIO

Listen, they've spotted another ship!

A gunshot is heard.

SECOND GENTLEMAN

They fired a greeting shot too, so this is also a friendly ship.

CASSIO

Go find out the news.

SECOND GENTLEMAN *exits.*

105   Good ancient, you are welcome.—Welcome, mistress.
(kisses EMILIA*)*
Let it not gall your patience, good Iago,
That I extend my manners. 'Tis my breeding
That gives me this bold show of courtesy.

IAGO

Sir, would she give you so much of her lips
110   As of her tongue she oft bestows on me,
You'll have enough.

DESDEMONA
Alas, she has no speech!

IAGO

In faith, too much.
I find it still, when I have leave to sleep.
115   Marry, before your ladyship, I grant,
She puts her tongue a little in her heart
And chides with thinking.

EMILIA

                    You have little cause to say so.

IAGO

Come on, come on. You are pictures out of door, bells in
your parlors, wild-cats in your kitchens, saints in your
120   injuries, devils being offended, players in your
housewifery, and housewives in your beds.

DESDEMONA
Oh, fie upon thee, slanderer!

IAGO

Nay, it is true, or else I am a Turk.
You rise to play and go to bed to work.

EMILIA
125   You shall not write my praise.

IAGO

                    No, let me not.

Ensign Iago, welcome.—And welcome to you, too, madam. *(he kisses* EMILIA*)* Don't be upset that I kissed your wife hello, Iago. It's a courtesy where I come from.

IAGO

If she gave you as much lip as she gives me, you'd be sick of her by now.

DESDEMONA

On the contrary, she's a soft-spoken woman.

IAGO

No, she talks too much. She's always talking when I want to sleep. I admit that in front of you, my lady, she keeps a bit quiet. But she's scolding me silently.

EMILIA

You have no reason to say that.

IAGO

Come on, come on. You women are all the same. You're as pretty as pictures when you're out in public, but in your own houses you're as noisy as jangling bells. In your own kitchens you act like wildcats. You make yourselves sound like saints when you're complaining about something, but you act like devils when someone offends you. You don't take your jobs as housewives seriously, and you're shameless hussies in bed.

DESDEMONA

Shame on you, you slanderer!

IAGO

No, it's true, or if it's not, I'm a villain. You wake up to have fun, and you start work when you go to bed.

EMILIA

You clearly have nothing good to say about me.

IAGO

No, I don't.

DESDEMONA

What wouldst thou write of me, if thou should'st
praise me?

IAGO

O gentle lady, do not put me to 't,
For I am nothing, if not critical.

DESDEMONA

130   Come on, assay. There's one gone to the harbor?

IAGO

Ay, madam.

DESDEMONA

I am not merry, but I do beguile
The thing I am by seeming otherwise.
Come, how wouldst thou praise me?

IAGO

135   I am about it, but indeed my invention
Comes from my pate as birdlime does from frieze,
It plucks out brains and all. But my Muse labors
And thus she is delivered:
If she be fair and wise, fairness and wit,
140   The one's for use, the other useth it.

DESDEMONA

Well praised! How if she be black and witty?

IAGO

If she be black, and thereto have a wit,
She'll find a white that shall her blackness fit.

DESDEMONA

Worse and worse!

EMILIA

                        How if fair and foolish?

IAGO

145   She never yet was foolish that was fair,
For even her folly helped her to an heir.

DESDEMONA

These are old fond paradoxes to make fools laugh i' th'
alehouse. What miserable praise hast thou for her
That's foul and foolish?

DESDEMONA

But if you had to say something nice about me, what would you say?

IAGO

Don't make me do it, my lady. I'm critical by nature.

DESDEMONA

Come on, just try.—By the way, has someone gone down to the harbor?

IAGO

Yes, madam.

DESDEMONA

I'm not as happy as I seem. I'm just trying not to show how worried I am about Othello's safety. Come on, what would you say about me?

IAGO

I'm trying to think of something, but I'm not good at inventing clever things. It takes time. Ah, I've got it. If a woman is pretty and smart, she uses her good looks to get what she wants.

DESDEMONA

Very clever! But what if the woman is smart but ugly?

IAGO

Even if she's ugly, she'll be smart enough to find a guy to sleep with her.

DESDEMONA

This is getting worse and worse!

EMILIA

What if she's pretty but stupid?

IAGO

No pretty woman is stupid, because her stupidity will make her more attractive to men.

DESDEMONA

These are stupid old jokes that men tell each other in bars. What horrible thing do you have to say about a woman who's both ugly and stupid?

IAGO

150   There's none so foul and foolish thereunto,
   But does foul pranks which fair and wise ones do.

DESDEMONA

   Oh, heavy ignorance! Thou praisest the worst best. But
   what praise couldst thou bestow on a deserving woman
   indeed, one that in the authority of her merit did justly put
155   on the vouch of very malice itself?

IAGO

   She that was ever fair and never proud,
   Had tongue at will and yet was never loud,
   Never lacked gold and yet went never gay,
   Fled from her wish and yet said "Now I may,"
160   She that being angered, her revenge being nigh,
   Bade her wrong stay and her displeasure fly,
   She that in wisdom never was so frail
   To change the cod's head for the salmon's tail,
   She that could think and ne'er disclose her mind,
165   See suitors following and not look behind,
   She was a wight, if ever such wights were—

DESDEMONA

   To do what?

IAGO

   To suckle fools and chronicle small beer.

DESDEMONA

   Oh, most lame and impotent conclusion! Do not learn of
170   him, Emilia, though he be thy husband. How say you,
   Cassio? Is he not a most profane and liberal counselor?

CASSIO

   He speaks home, madam. You may relish him more in the
   soldier than in the scholar.

   CASSIO *takes* DESDEMONA'S *hand*

IAGO

   (aside) He takes her by the palm. Ay, well said, whisper!
175.   With as little a web as this will I ensnare as great a fly as

IAGO

No matter how ugly or stupid the woman is, she plays the same dirty tricks that the smart and pretty ones do.

DESDEMONA

You don't know a thing! You give your best praise to the worst women. But how would you praise a truly good woman, someone who had no reason to worry about what anyone said about her?

IAGO

A woman who was beautiful but never proud, who could speak well but knew when to be quiet, who dressed well but was never overdressed, who had self-restraint even when she could get what she wanted, a woman who never took revenge, who overlooked it when people hurt her, who was too wise to do anything stupid, who could think without revealing her thoughts, and who could refrain from flirting with men in love with her, that kind of woman, if she ever existed, would—

DESDEMONA

Would do what?

IAGO

Would raise babies and clip coupons.

DESDEMONA

Oh, that's pathetic! Don't listen to him, Emilia, even though he's your husband. What do you think about him, Cassio? Isn't he a horrible man?

CASSIO

He speaks bluntly, madam. He's more of a soldier than a wise man.

CASSIO *takes* DESDEMONA'S *hand.*

IAGO

(to himself) He's taking her hand. That's right, go ahead and whisper together. This is all I need to get

Cassio. Ay, smile upon her, do, I will gyve thee in thine own courtship. You say true, 'Tis so, indeed. If such tricks as these strip you out of your lieutenantry, it had been better you had not kissed your three fingers so oft, which now again you are

180   most apt to play the sir in. Very good, well kissed, and excellent courtesy! 'tis so, indeed. Yet again your fingers to your lips? Would they were clyster-pipes for your sake!—

Trumpet within

The Moor! I know his trumpet.

CASSIO

                                   'Tis truly so.

DESDEMONA

Let's meet him and receive him.

CASSIO

                             Lo, where he comes!

Enter OTHELLO *and attendants*

OTHELLO

185   Oh my fair warrior!

DESDEMONA

                       My dear Othello!

OTHELLO

It gives me wonder great as my content
To see you here before me. Oh, my soul's joy!
If after every tempest come such calms,
May the winds blow till they have wakened death,

190   And let the laboring bark climb hills of seas
Olympus-high, and duck again as low
As hell's from heaven! If it were now to die,
'Twere now to be most happy, for I fear
My soul hath her content so absolute

195   That not another comfort like to this
Succeeds in unknown fate.

Cassio. Yes, keep smiling at her, Cassio. Your fine manners around women will be your downfall. Oh, I'm sure you're saying something very clever. If you lose your job because of little flirtations like this, you'll wish you hadn't been so courteous with her. Oh, how nice, you're kissing your own hand, one finger at a time? I wish those fingers were enema tubes!—

A gentleman's kissing his own fingers was considered a polite gesture.

A trumpet plays offstage.

That's the Moor! I recognize his trumpet.

CASSIO
Yes, it is.

DESDEMONA
Let's go greet him when he lands.

CASSIO
Look, here he comes.

OTHELLO *enters with attendants.*

OTHELLO
My beautiful warrior!

DESDEMONA
My darling Othello!

OTHELLO
I'm amazed you got here before me. But I'm overjoyed! My love, if the calm after the storm could always be this wonderful, I'd want the wind to blow until it waked the dead, and whipped up waves as tall as mountains! If I died right now I'd be completely happy, since I'll probably never be as happy as this again in my life.

DESDEMONA

                       The heavens forbid
But that our loves and comforts should increase,
Even as our days do grow.

OTHELLO

                    Amen to that, sweet powers!
I cannot speak enough of this content.
200   It stops me here, it is too much of joy.
And this, and this, the greatest discords be *(kissing her)*
That e'er our hearts shall make!

IAGO

(aside)

                   Oh, you are well tuned now,
But I'll set down the pegs that make this music,
As honest as I am.

OTHELLO

                Come, let us to the castle.
205   News, friends! Our wars are done, the Turks
           are drowned.
How does my old acquaintance of this isle?—
Honey, you shall be well desired in Cyprus,
I have found great love amongst them. O my sweet,
I prattle out of fashion, and I dote
210   In mine own comforts.—I prithee, good Iago,
Go to the bay and disembark my coffers.
Bring thou the master to the citadel.
He is a good one, and his worthiness
Does challenge much respect.—Come, Desdemona,
215   Once more, well met at Cyprus.

              Exeunt OTHELLO, DESDEMONA, *and attendants*

IAGO

Do thou meet me presently at the harbor.—Come hither.
If thou be'st valiant, as they say base men being in love
have then a nobility in their natures more than is native to
them, list me. The lieutenant tonight watches on the court

DESDEMONA

God willing, our love and our happiness will only increase as we get older.

OTHELLO

Amen to that! I can't talk about my happiness anymore. It's too much. I hope these kisses I'm about to give you are the closest we ever come to fighting. *(they kiss)*

IAGO

(to himself) Oh, you're happy now, but I'll ruin your happiness, for all my supposed honesty.

OTHELLO

Let's go up to the castle. Good news, friends. The war's over and the Turks are drowned. How are my old friends from this island doing?—Honey, they'll love you here in Cyprus. They've been very good to me here. Oh, my dear, I'm blabbing on and on because I'm so happy.—Iago, would you be good enough to go get my trunks from the ships? And bring the ship's captain to the castle. He's a good man.—Let's go, Desdemona. I'll say it again: I'm so happy to see you here in Cyprus!

OTHELLO, DESDEMONA, *and attendants exit.*

IAGO

Meet me down at the harbor.—Come here. They say love makes cowards brave. So if you're brave, listen to me. Lieutenant Cassio will be on guard duty tonight.

220   of guard. First, I must tell thee this: Desdemona is directly
        in love with him.

RODERIGO
        With him? Why, 'tis not possible.

IAGO
        Lay thy finger thus, and let thy soul be instructed. Mark
        me with what violence she first loved the Moor, but for
225   bragging and telling her fantastical lies. To love him still
        for prating? Let not thy discreet heart think it. Her eye
        must be fed, and what delight shall she have to look on the
        devil? When the blood is made dull with the act of sport,
        there should be a game to inflame it and to give satiety a
230   fresh appetite, loveliness in favor, sympathy in years,
        manners and beauties. All which the Moor is defective in.
        Now for want of these required conveniences, her delicate
        tenderness will find itself abused, begin to heave the gorge,
        disrelish and abhor the Moor. Very nature will instruct
235   her in it and compel her to some second choice. Now sir,
        this granted—as it is a most pregnant and unforced
        position—who stands so eminent in the degree of this
        fortune as Cassio does? A knave very voluble, no further
        conscionable than in putting on the mere form of civil and
240   humane seeming, for the better compassing of his salt and
        most hidden loose affection. Why, none, why, none! A
        slipper and subtle knave, a finder of occasions that has an
        eye, can stamp and counterfeit advantages, though true
        advantage never present itself. A devilish knave. Besides,
245   the knave is handsome, young, and hath all those requisites
        in him that folly and green minds look after. A pestilent
        complete knave, and the woman hath found him already.

RODERIGO
        I cannot believe that in her. She's full of most blessed
        condition.

IAGO
250.   Blessed fig's-end! The wine she drinks is made of grapes.
        If she had been blessed, she would never have loved the

But first, I have to tell you that Desdemona's completely in love with him.

RODERIGO

With Cassio? That's impossible.

IAGO

Be quiet and listen to me. Remember how she fell madly in love with the Moor because he bragged and told her made-up stories? Did you expect her to keep on loving him for his chattering? You're too smart to think that. No, she needs someone nice-looking. Othello's ugly, what pleasure could she find in him? Lovemaking gets boring after a while. To keep things hot, she'll need to see someone with a handsome face, someone close to her in age, someone who looks and acts like her. Othello isn't any of those things. Since he doesn't have these advantages to make him attractive to her, she'll get sick of him until he makes her want to puke. She'll start looking around for a second choice. Now, if that's true—and it's obviously true—who's in a better position than Cassio? He's a smooth talker, and uses sophistication and fine manners to hide his lust. Nobody's as crafty as he is. Besides, he's young and handsome, and he's got all the qualities that naïve and silly girls go for. He's a bad boy, and Desdemona's got her eye on him already.

RODERIGO

I can't believe that. She's not that kind of woman. She's very moral.

IAGO

Like hell she is! She's made of the same flesh and blood as everyone else. If she were so moral, she would never have fallen in love with the Moor in the first place.

Moor. Blessed pudding! Didst thou not see her paddle
with the palm of his hand? Didst not mark that?

RODERIGO

Yes, that I did, but that was but courtesy.

IAGO

255 Lechery, by this hand, an index and obscure prologue to
the history of lust and foul thoughts. They met so near
with their lips that their breaths embraced together.
Villainous thoughts, Roderigo! When these mutabilities
so marshal the way, hard at hand comes the master and
260 main exercise, th' incorporate conclusion. Pish! But, sir,
be you ruled by me. I have brought you from Venice.
Watch you tonight for the command, I'll lay 't upon you.
Cassio knows you not. I'll not be far from you. Do you
find some occasion to anger Cassio, either by speaking too
265 loud, or tainting his discipline, or from what other course
you please, which the time shall more favorably minister.

RODERIGO

Well.

IAGO

Sir, he's rash and very sudden in choler, and haply may
strike at you. Provoke him that he may. For even out of that
270 will I cause these of Cyprus to mutiny, whose qualification
shall come into no true taste again but by the displanting of
Cassio. So shall you have a shorter journey to your desires
by the means I shall then have to prefer them, and the
impediment most profitably removed, without the
275 which there were no expectation of our prosperity.

RODERIGO

I will do this, if you can bring it to any opportunity.

IAGO

I warrant thee. Meet me by and by at the citadel. I must
fetch his necessaries ashore. Farewell.

RODERIGO

Adieu.

Exit

Good lord! Did you notice how she and Cassio were fondling each other's hands? Did you see that?

RODERIGO

Yes, I did. But that wasn't romantic, it was just polite manners.

IAGO

They were lusting after each other. You could tell by how they were acting that they're going to be lovers. They were so close that their breath was mingling. When two people get that intimate, sex will soon follow. Disgusting! But listen to me; let me guide you. I brought you here from Venice. Be on guard duty tonight. I'll put you in charge. Cassio doesn't know you. I'll be nearby. Make Cassio angry somehow, either by speaking too loud, or insulting his military skills, or however else you want.

RODERIGO

All right.

IAGO

He's hot-tempered, and he might try to hit you with his staff. Try to get him to do that. That'll allow me to stir up public sentiment against him here in Cyprus. I'll get them so riled up that they'll only calm down when Cassio's fired. To get what you want, you need to get Cassio out of the way. If you don't do that, things are hopeless for you.

RODERIGO

I'll do it, if you help me out.

IAGO

I promise I will. Meet me in a little while at the citadel. I need to get Othello's things from the ship. Goodbye.

RODERIGO

Goodbye.

RODERIGO *exits.*

IAGO

280   That Cassio loves her, I do well believe 't.
       That she loves him, 'tis apt and of great credit.
       The Moor, howbeit that I endure him not,
       Is of a constant, loving, noble nature,
       And I dare think he'll prove to Desdemona
285   A most dear husband. Now, I do love her too,
       Not out of absolute lust—though peradventure
       I stand accountant for as great a sin—
       But partly led to diet my revenge,
       For that I do suspect the lusty Moor
290   Hath leaped into my seat. The thought whereof
       Doth, like a poisonous mineral, gnaw my inwards,
       And nothing can or shall content my soul
       Till I am evened with him, wife for wife.
       Or, failing so, yet that I put the Moor
295   At least into a jealousy so strong
       That judgment cannot cure. Which thing to do,
       If this poor trash of Venice, whom I trace
       For his quick hunting, stand the putting on,
       I'll have our Michael Cassio on the hip,
300   Abuse him to the Moor in the right garb
       (For I fear Cassio with my night-cape too)
       Make the Moor thank me, love me, and reward me
       For making him egregiously an ass
       And practicing upon his peace and quiet
305   Even to madness. 'Tis here, but yet confused.
       Knavery's plain face is never seen till used.

                                                        Exit

IAGO

I think Cassio really does love her, and it's perfectly likely that she loves him too. I can't stand the Moor, but I have to admit that he's a reliable, loving, and good-natured man. He'd probably be a good husband to Desdemona. I love her too, not simply out of lust, but also to feed my revenge. I have a feeling the Moor slept with my wife. That thought keeps gnawing at me, eating me up inside. I won't be satisfied until I get even with him, wife for wife. If I can't do that, I can at least make the Moor so jealous that he can't think straight. If that piece of Venetian trash Roderigo can do what I need to carry out my plan, I'll have power over Cassio. I'll say bad things about him to the Moor. I have a feeling Cassio seduced my wife as well. I'll make the Moor thank me, love me, and reward me, even though the joke will be on him the whole time. I've got a good plan, though I haven't worked out the details yet. You can never see the end of an evil plan until the moment comes.

IAGO exits.

ACT 2, SCENE 2

Enter Othello's HERALD, *with a proclamation*

HERALD
It is Othello's pleasure, our noble and valiant general,
that, upon certain tidings now arrived, importing the
mere perdition of the Turkish fleet, every man put himself
into triumph: some to dance, some to make bonfires, each
5   man to what sport and revels his addiction leads him. For
besides these beneficial news, it is the celebration of his
nuptial. So much was his pleasure should be proclaimed.
All offices are open, and there is full liberty of feasting
from this present hour of five till the bell have told eleven.
10   Bless the isle of Cyprus and our noble general Othello!

Exit

ACT 2, SCENE 2

Othello's HERALD *enters with a proclamation.*

HERALD

Our noble and courageous general Othello having been informed that the Turkish fleet has been completely destroyed, invites every man to celebrate our victory. Some of you dance, some of you make bonfires, and every man celebrate in whatever way he likes to. For besides the good news, we are also celebrating his marriage. That's the end of the announcement. There will be a feast from five o'clock until eleven. God bless the island of Cyprus and our noble general Othello!

The HERALD *exits.*

ACT 2, SCENE 3

Enter OTHELLO, DESDEMONA, CASSIO, *and attendants*

OTHELLO
> Good Michael, look you to the guard tonight.
> Let's teach ourselves that honorable stop
> Not to outsport discretion.

CASSIO
> Iago hath direction what to do,
5 > But notwithstanding with my personal eye
> Will I look to 't.

OTHELLO
>   Iago is most honest.
> Michael, good night. Tomorrow with your earliest
> Let me have speech with you.—
> Come, my dear love,
10 > The purchase made, the fruits are to ensue:
> That profit's yet to come 'tween me and you.
> Good night.

> *Exeunt* OTHELLO, DESDEMONA, *and attendants*
> *Enter* IAGO

CASSIO
> Welcome, Iago. We must to the watch.

IAGO
> Not this hour, lieutenant, 'tis not yet ten o' the clock. Our
15 > general cast us thus early for the love of his Desdemona—
> who let us not therefore blame. He hath not yet made
> wanton the night with her, and she is sport for Jove.

CASSIO
> She's a most exquisite lady.

IAGO
> And, I'll warrant her, full of game.

ACT 2, SCENE 3

OTHELLO, DESDEMONA, CASSIO *and attendants enter.*

OTHELLO

Good Michael, keep a careful eye on the guards tonight. Let's exercise restraint and not let the party get too wild.

CASSIO

Iago has orders what to do. But I'll see to it personally anyway.

OTHELLO

Iago's a good man. Goodnight, Michael. Come talk to me tomorrow as early as you can.—Come with me, my dear love. Now that the wedding's over, we can have the pleasure of consummating our marriage. Good night, everyone.

OTHELLO *and* DESDEMONA *exit with their attendants.* IAGO *enters.*

CASSIO

Hello, Iago. It's time for us to stand guard.

IAGO

Jove is the head of the gods in Roman mythology

Not yet, lieutenant. It's not even ten o'clock. The general got rid of us early tonight so he could be with Desdemona.—I can't blame him. He hasn't spent the night with her yet, and she's beautiful enough to be Jove's lover.

CASSIO

She's an exquisitely beautiful lady.

IAGO

And I bet she's good in bed too.

CASSIO

20   Indeed she's a most fresh and delicate creature.

IAGO

What an eye she has! Methinks it sounds a parley to
provocation.

CASSIO

An inviting eye, and yet methinks right modest.

IAGO

And when she speaks, is it not an alarum to love?

CASSIO

25   She is indeed perfection.

IAGO

Well, happiness to their sheets! Come, lieutenant, I have
a stoup of wine, and here without are a brace of Cyprus
gallants that would fain have a measure to the health of
black Othello.

CASSIO

30   Not tonight, good Iago. I have very poor and unhappy
brains for drinking. I could well wish courtesy would
invent some other custom of entertainment.

IAGO

Oh, they are our friends. But one cup. I'll drink for you.

CASSIO

I have drunk but one cup tonight, and that was craftily
35   qualified too, and behold what innovation it makes here.
I am unfortunate in the infirmity, and dare not task my
weakness with any more.

IAGO

What, man, 'tis a night of revels! The gallants desire it.

CASSIO

Where are they?

IAGO

40   Here at the door. I pray you call them in.

CASSIO

I'll do 't, but it dislikes me.

Exit

CASSIO

Yes, she's young and tender.

IAGO

And such pretty eyes! Like an invitation.

CASSIO

Yes, she's pretty. But she's modest and ladylike too.

IAGO

And when she speaks, doesn't her voice stir up passion?

CASSIO

She's a perfect woman, it's true.

IAGO

Well, good luck to them tonight in bed! Come with us, lieutenant. I've got a jug of wine, and these two Cyprus gentlemen want to drink a toast to the black Othello.

CASSIO

Not tonight, Iago. I'm not much of a drinker. I wish there was less social pressure to drink.

IAGO

Oh, but these are our friends. Just one glass. I'll do most of the drinking for you.

CASSIO

I've already had a glass of wine tonight, watered down, but look how drunk I am. I'm not a heavy drinker. I wouldn't dare drink much more than that.

IAGO

What are you talking about, man? Tonight is for celebrating! The gentlemen are waiting.

CASSIO

Where are they?

IAGO

By the door. Please invite them in.

CASSIO

I'll do it, but I don't like it.

CASSIO exits.

IAGO
If I can fasten but one cup upon him,
With that which he hath drunk tonight already,
He'll be as full of quarrel and offense
45 As my young mistress' dog. Now my sick fool Roderigo,
Whom love hath turned almost the wrong side out,
To Desdemona hath tonight caroused
Potations pottle-deep, and he's to watch.
Three lads of Cyprus, noble swelling spirits
50 (That hold their honors in a wary distance,
The very elements of this warlike isle)
Have I tonight flustered with flowing cups,
And they watch too. Now 'mongst this flock of drunkards
Am I to put our Cassio in some action
55 That may offend the isle.
                                    But here they come.
If consequence do but approve my dream
My boat sails freely, both with wind and stream.

Enter CASSIO, MONTANO *and gentlemen*

CASSIO
'Fore heaven, they have given me a rouse already.
MONTANO
Good faith, a little one, not past a pint,
60 As I am a soldier.
IAGO
                                    Some wine, ho!
(sings)
        And let me the cannikin clink, clink,
        And let me the cannikin clink.
        A soldier's a man,
        A life's but a span,
65   *Why then let a soldier drink.*
        Some wine, boys!

IAGO

If I can just get him to drink one more glass after what he's drunk already, he'll be as argumentative and eager to fight as a little dog. That fool Roderigo, all twisted up inside with love, has been drinking toasts to Desdemona by the gallon, and he's on guard duty. I've gotten the rest of the guards drunk, as well as several gentlemen from Cyprus who are quick to take offense. Now I'll get Cassio to do something in front of all these drunkards that will offend everyone on the island. Here they come. If the future turns out as I hope it will, I'm all set for success.

CASSIO, MONTANO, *and* GENTLEMEN *enter, followed by servants with wine.*

CASSIO

My God, they've given me a lot to drink.

MONTANO

No, it was a little one, not more than a pint.

IAGO

Bring in more wine!
(he sings)
> And clink your glasses together,
> And clink your glasses together.
> A soldier's a man,
> And a man's life is short,
> So let the soldier drink.
> Have some more wine, boys!

CASSIO

'Fore heaven, an excellent song.

IAGO

I learned it in England where indeed they are most potent in potting. Your Dane, your German, and your swag-bellied
70   Hollander—Drink, ho!—are nothing to your English.

CASSIO

Is your Englishman so expert in his drinking?

IAGO

Why, he drinks you with facility your Dane dead drunk; he sweats not to overthrow your Almain. He gives your Hollander a vomit ere the next pottle can be filled.

CASSIO

75   To the health of our general!

MONTANO

I am for it, lieutenant, and I'll do you justice.

IAGO

Oh, sweet England!

(sings)

> *King Stephen was a worthy peer,*
> *His breeches cost him but a crown,*
80   > *He held them sixpence all too dear,*
> *With that he called the tailor lown.*
> *He was a wight of high renown,*
> *And thou art but of low degree,*
> *'Tis pride that pulls the country down,*
85   > *Then take thine auld cloak about thee.*
> *Some wine, ho!*

CASSIO

Why, this is a more exquisite song than the other.

IAGO

Will you hear 't again?

CASSIO

No, for I hold him to be unworthy of his place that does
90   those things. Well, heaven's above all, and there be souls must be saved, and there be souls must not be saved.

IAGO

It's true, good lieutenant.

CASSIO

My God, what a great song!

IAGO

I learned it England, where they have a talent for drinking. The Danes, the Germans, and the Dutch—come on, drink, drink!—are nothing compared to the English.

CASSIO

Are Englishmen really such heavy drinkers?

IAGO

They drink Danes under the table, and it takes them no effort at all to out-drink Germans. And the Dutch are vomiting while the English are asking for refills.

CASSIO

Let's drink to our general!

MONTANO

Hear, hear! I'll drink as much as you do!

IAGO

Oh, sweet England!
(he sings)
    King Stephen was a good king, and his pants were
        very cheap,
    But he thought his tailor overcharged him, so he
        called him a peasant.
    And that was a man of noble rank, much higher than
        you are.
    So be happy with your worn-out cloak,
    Since pride is ruining the nation.
    More wine!

CASSIO

God, that song's even better than the other one.

IAGO

Do you want to hear it again?

CASSIO

No, because we shouldn't be doing that— stuff. Oh well, God's in charge, and some people have to go to heaven, while other people have to go to hell.

IAGO

That's true, lieutenant.

CASSIO

For mine own part, no offence to the general nor any man
of quality, I hope to be saved.

IAGO

95   And so do I too, lieutenant.

CASSIO

Ay, but (by your leave) not before me. The lieutenant is to
be saved before the ancient. Let's have no more of this,
let's to our affairs.—Forgive us our sins!—Gentlemen,
let's look to our business. Do not think, gentlemen, I am
100 drunk. This is my ancient, this is my right hand, and this
is my left. I am not drunk now. I can stand well enough,
and I speak well enough.

ALL

Excellent well!

CASSIO

Why, very well then. You must not think then that I am
105 drunk.

Exit

MONTANO

To th' platform, masters. Come, let's set the watch.

Exit GENTLEMEN

IAGO

You see this fellow that is gone before,
He is a soldier fit to stand by Caesar
And give direction. And do but see his vice,
110 'Tis to his virtue a just equinox,
The one as long as th' other. 'Tis pity of him.
I fear the trust Othello puts him in
On some odd time of his infirmity
Will shake this island.

MONTANO

                                   But is he often thus?

CASSIO

Speaking for myself—and no offense to the general or anyone else—I hope I'm going to heaven.

IAGO

Me too, lieutenant.

CASSIO

Okay, but please not before me. The lieutenant has to get to heaven before the ensign. But let's stop this drinking and get down to business.—God forgive our sins!—Gentlemen, let's get down to business. By the way, I don't want anyone thinking I'm drunk. This is my ensign. This is my right hand, and this is my left hand.

I'm not drunk. I can stand well enough, and I can speak just fine.

ALL

Yes, you're speaking very well.

CASSIO

Yes, very well. So don't think that I'm drunk.

CASSIO exits.

MONTANO

Let's go to the platform where we'll stand guard. Come on.

GENTLEMEN exit.

IAGO

You see that man who just left? He's a good soldier, good enough to be Caesar's right-hand man. But he has a serious weakness. It's too bad. I'm worried that Othello trusts him too much, and it'll be bad for Cyprus eventually.

MONTANO

But is he often like this?

IAGO

115   'Tis evermore the prologue to his sleep.
He'll watch the horologe a double set
If drink rock not his cradle.

MONTANO

                  It were well
The general were put in mind of it.
Perhaps he sees it not, or his good nature

120   Prizes the virtue that appears in Cassio
And looks not on his evils. Is not this true?

Enter RODERIGO

IAGO

(aside) How now, Roderigo?
I pray you, after the lieutenant, go!

                        Exit RODERIGO

MONTANO

And 'tis great pity that the noble Moor

125   Should hazard such a place as his own second
With one of an ingraft infirmity.
It were an honest action to say
So to the Moor.

IAGO

             Not I, for this fair island.
I do love Cassio well, and would do much

130   To cure him of this evil—

Cry within "Help! help!"

IAGO

But, hark! What noise?

Enter CASSIO, *pursuing* RODERIGO

IAGO

He drinks like this every night before he goes to sleep. He'd stay up all night and all day if he didn't drink himself to sleep.

MONTANO

The general should be informed about this. Maybe he's never noticed, or he only wants to see Cassio's good side. Don't you think so?

RODERIGO *enters.*

IAGO

(*speaking so that only* RODERIGO *can hear*) Hello, Roderigo. Please, follow the lieutenant. Hurry! Go!

RODERIGO *exits.*

MONTANO

And it's too bad that the Moor chose a man with such a deep-rooted drinking problem as his second-in-command. We should definitely say something to the Moor.

IAGO

I wouldn't say anything, not if you gave me the whole island for doing so. I respect Cassio and I'd like to help cure his alcoholism—

A voice offstage calls "Help! Help!"

IAGO

What's that noise?

CASSIO *enters, chasing* RODERIGO.

CASSIO
Zounds! You rogue! You rascal!

MONTANO
What's the matter, lieutenant?

CASSIO
A knave teach me my duty?

135   I'll beat the knave into a twiggen bottle.

RODERIGO
Beat me?

CASSIO
Dost thou prate, rogue? *(strikes him)*

MONTANO
Nay, good lieutenant! I pray you, sir, hold your hand.
(stays him)

CASSIO
Let me go, sir, or I'll knock you o'er the mazzard.

MONTANO
140   Come, come, you're drunk.

CASSIO
Drunk?

They fight

IAGO
(aside to RODERIGO)
Away, I say, go out, and cry a mutiny.—

Exit RODERIGO

Nay, good lieutenant! Alas, gentlemen—
Help, ho!— Lieutenant—sir, Montano—
145   Help, masters!—Here's a goodly watch indeed!

Bell rings

CASSIO

Damn you, you villain, you rascal!

MONTANO

What's the matter, lieutenant?

CASSIO

To think that fool had the nerve to try to teach me manners! I'll beat him until the welts look like basket-weave!

RODERIGO

You'll beat me?

CASSIO

Are you talking, you villain? *(he hits* RODERIGO*)*

MONTANO

No, don't hit him, lieutenant! Please, sir, restrain yourself. *(he restrains* CASSIO*)*

CASSIO

Let me go, or I'll knock you on the head.

MONTANO

Come on, you're drunk.

CASSIO

Drunk?

MONTANO *and* CASSIO *fight.*

IAGO

(speaking so that only RODERIGO *can hear)* Go tell everyone there's a riot.—

RODERIGO *exits.*

No, lieutenant—God, gentlemen—Help—Lieutenant—sir, Montano—Help, men!—The night guard is coming!

Someone rings a bell.

Who's that which rings the bell?—Diablo, ho!
The town will rise. Fie, Fie, lieutenant,
You'll be ashamed for ever.

Enter OTHELLO *and attendants*

OTHELLO
What is the matter here?

MONTANO
150   I bleed still,
I am hurt to the death. He dies!

OTHELLO
Hold, for your lives!

IAGO
Hold, ho! Lieutenant—sir, Montano—gentlemen,
Have you forgot all place of sense and duty?
155   Hold! The general speaks to you. Hold, for shame!

OTHELLO
Why, how now, ho! From whence ariseth this?
Are we turned Turks? And to ourselves do that
Which heaven hath forbid the Ottomites?
For Christian shame, put by this barbarous brawl.
160   He that stirs next to carve for his own rage
Holds his soul light, he dies upon his motion.
Silence that dreadful bell, it frights the isle
From her propriety. What is the matter, masters?—
Honest Iago, that looks dead with grieving,
165   Speak, who began this? On thy love, I charge thee.

IAGO
I do not know. Friends all but now, even now,
In quarter, and in terms like bride and groom
Divesting them for bed. And then, but now,
As if some planet had unwitted men,

Who's sounding that alarm? The whole town will riot!
God, lieutenant, please stop! You'll be ashamed of this
forever!

OTHELLO *enters with attendants.*

OTHELLO

What is the matter here?

MONTANO

My God, I'm bleeding! I've been mortally wounded.
I'll kill him!

OTHELLO

Stop right now!

IAGO

Stop! Lieutenant—sir, Montano—gentlemen! Have
you forgotten your duty and your sense of decorum?
Stop! The general is talking to you! Stop, for God's
sake!

OTHELLO

How did this all start? Have we all become as savage as
the Turks, treating each other as badly as they would
have treated us? For heaven's sake, stop this savage
brawl! The next man who swings his sword must not
care about his life, because the instant he strikes, he
dies. Stop that alarm from ringing, it's scaring the
islanders. What's the matter here, gentlemen?—Honest Iago, you look upset. Speak up and tell me who
started this. Answer me.

IAGO

I don't know. We were all having fun until just a
minute ago; we were as happy as a bride and groom
taking off their clothes. But then the mood suddenly
changed. It was as if something had driven the men

170   Swords out, and tilting one at other's breasts
        In opposition bloody. I cannot speak
        Any beginning to this peevish odds,
        And would in action glorious I had lost
        Those legs that brought me to a part of it.

OTHELLO
175   How comes it, Michael, you are thus forgot?

CASSIO
        I pray you pardon me, I cannot speak.

OTHELLO
        Worthy Montano, you were wont be civil.
        The gravity and stillness of your youth
        The world hath noted, and your name is great
180   In mouths of wisest censure. What's the matter
        That you unlace your reputation thus
        And spend your rich opinion for the name
        Of a night-brawler? Give me answer to it.

MONTANO
        Worthy Othello, I am hurt to danger.
185   Your officer Iago can inform you,
        While I spare speech, which something now offends me,
        Of all that I do know. Nor know I aught
        By me that's said or done amiss this night,
        Unless self-charity be sometimes a vice,
190   And to defend ourselves it be a sin
        When violence assails us.

OTHELLO
                                Now, by heaven,
        My blood begins my safer guides to rule,
        And passion, having my best judgment collied,
        Assays to lead the way. If I once stir,

insane and made them point their swords at one another. I don't know what could have started this. I'd rather have lost my legs in battle than be a part of this!

OTHELLO

How did you manage to lose your self-control like this, Michael?

CASSIO

Please, excuse me, sir. I can't speak.

OTHELLO

Montano, you're supposed to be calm and collected. You're famous for it. Wise people respect you. What in the world made you risk your reputation like this and become a street brawler? Tell me.

MONTANO

Othello, I've been seriously hurt. Your officer Iago can tell you what happened. I should save my breath, since it hurts to talk. I didn't do anything wrong that I know of, unless it was a sin to defend myself when someone attacked me.

OTHELLO

All right, now I'm starting to lose my cool.
By God, if you don't tell me what happened you'll all suffer. Tell me how this fight began, who started it. Whoever is guilty, even if he were my twin brother, I

195   Or do but lift this arm, the best of you
       Shall sink in my rebuke. Give me to know
       How this foul rout began, who set it on,
       And he that is approved in this offence,
       Though he had twinned with me, both at a birth,
200   Shall lose me. What, in a town of war
       Yet wild, the people's hearts brimful of fear,
       To manage private and domestic quarrel?
       In night, and on the court and guard of safety?
       'Tis monstrous. Iago, who began 't?

MONTANO

205   If partially affined or leagued in office
       Thou dost deliver more or less than truth
       Thou art no soldier.

IAGO

                           Touch me not so near.
       I had rather have this tongue cut from my mouth
       Than it should do offence to Michael Cassio.
210   Yet I persuade myself to speak the truth
       Shall nothing wrong him. This it is, general:
       Montano and myself being in speech,
       There comes a fellow crying out for help
       And Cassio following him with determined sword
215   To execute upon him. Sir, this gentleman
       Steps in to Cassio and entreats his pause,
       Myself the crying fellow did pursue,
       Lest by his clamor—as it so fell out—
       The town might fall in fright. He, swift of foot,
220   Outran my purpose, and I returned then rather
       For that I heard the clink and fall of swords
       And Cassio high in oath, which till tonight
       I ne'er might say before. When I came back—
       For this was brief— I found them close together
225   At blow and thrust, even as again they were
       When you yourself did part them.
       More of this matter cannot I report.

swear I'm through with him. We're in a town that's just avoided a war, everyone's still on edge, and you're getting into private fights while you're supposed to be on guard duty? That's unbelievably bad. Iago, who started it?

MONTANO

I know you're close to Cassio, but if you diverge from the truth in any way, you're not a true soldier.

IAGO

You're hitting close to home there. I'd rather cut my tongue out of my mouth than say anything bad about Michael Cassio. But I don't think it'll hurt him to tell the truth. This is what happened, General. Montano and I were talking when a man came running, crying for help. Cassio was chasing him with his sword out, trying to kill the guy. This gentleman stopped Cassio and told him to put away his sword. I followed the guy who was crying for help, to keep him from scaring the public. But he was fast and outran me. When I got back, I heard the swords clinking and Cassio swearing. I'd never heard him swear before. They were nearly killing each other, as you saw when you pulled them apart. I can't tell you anything else.

But men are men, the best sometimes forget.
Though Cassio did some little wrong to him,
230   As men in rage strike those that wish them best,
Yet surely Cassio, I believe, received
From him that fled some strange indignity
Which patience could not pass.

OTHELLO

I know, Iago,
Thy honesty and love doth mince this matter,
235   Making it light to Cassio. Cassio, I love thee
But never more be officer of mine.—

Enter DESDEMONA, *attended*

Look, if my gentle love be not raised up!
I'll make thee an example.

DESDEMONA
What's the matter, dear?

OTHELLO
240   All's well, sweeting,
Come away to bed.—*(to* MONTANO*)* Sir, for your hurts
Myself will be your surgeon. Lead him off.

MONTANO *is led off*

Iago, look with care about the town
And silence those whom this vile brawl distracted.—
245   Come, Desdemona, 'tis the soldiers' life
To have their balmy slumbers waked with strife.

Exeunt all but IAGO *and* CASSIO

IAGO
What, are you hurt, lieutenant?

CASSIO
Ay, past all surgery.

IAGO
Marry, heaven forbid!

But nobody's perfect, and even the best man sometimes loses control and strikes out in rage. Cassio was wrong to hurt Montano, who was only trying to help him, but I'm sure the guy who ran away must have offended Cassio in some terrible way, and Cassio couldn't let it pass.

OTHELLO

Iago, I know you're fond of Cassio and are downplaying this for his benefit. Cassio, I love you, but you're never again going to be one of my officers.—

DESDEMONA *enters with attendants.*

Look, you've woken my wife! I'll make you an example for the others to learn from.

DESDEMONA

What's the matter, dear?

OTHELLO

Everything's fine, now, sweetheart. Go back to bed.— *(to* MONTANO*)* I'll see to it personally that your wounds are treated. Lead him off.

MONTANO *is carried off.*

Iago, go and calm down the townspeople.—Come with me, Desdemona. Unfortunately, it's part of the soldier's life to be woken up by trouble.

Everyone except CASSIO *and* IAGO *exits.*

IAGO

Are you hurt, lieutenant?

CASSIO

Yes, but no doctor can help me.

IAGO

Oh I hope that's not true!

CASSIO

250 Reputation, reputation, reputation! Oh, I have lost my
reputation! I have lost the immortal part of myself, and
what remains is bestial. My reputation, Iago, my
reputation!

IAGO

As I am an honest man, I thought you had received some
255 bodily wound. There is more sense in that than in
reputation. Reputation is an idle and most false
imposition, oft got without merit and lost without
deserving. You have lost no reputation at all unless you
repute yourself such a loser. What, man, there are ways to
260 recover the general again. You are but now cast in his
mood, a punishment more in policy than in malice, even
so as one would beat his offenseless dog to affright an
imperious lion. Sue to him again and he's yours.

CASSIO

I will rather sue to be despised than to deceive so good a
265 commander with so slight, so drunken, and so indiscreet
an officer. Drunk? And speak parrot? And squabble?
Swagger? Swear? And discourse fustian with one's own
shadow? O thou invisible spirit of wine, if thou hast no
name to be known by, let us call thee devil!

IAGO

270 What was he that you followed with your sword? What
had he done to you?

CASSIO

I know not.

IAGO

Is 't possible?

CASSIO

I remember a mass of things, but nothing distinctly. A
275 quarrel, but nothing wherefore. Oh, that men should put
an enemy in their mouths to steal away their brains! That
we should, with joy, pleasance revel and applause,
transform ourselves into beasts!

CASSIO

My reputation, my reputation! I've lost my reputation, the longest-living and truest part of myself! Everything else in me is just animal-like. Oh, my reputation, Iago, my reputation!

IAGO

I swear I thought you meant you'd been hurt physically. Your physical health matters more than your reputation. A reputation is a useless and fake quality that others impose on us. You haven't lost it unless you think you have. There are lots of ways to get on the general's good side again. You've been discharged because he's angry, and because he's obliged to do so for policy reasons, not because he dislikes you. He's got to beat up the weak to frighten the strong. Go to him, petition him. He'll change his mind.

CASSIO

I'd rather ask him to hate me than ask such a good commander to accept such a worthless, drunk, stupid officer as myself. Drunk? Babbling senselessly? Squabbling? Swaggering? Swearing? Ranting and raving to my own shadow! Oh, wine is the devil!

IAGO

Who were you chasing with your sword? What did he do to you?

CASSIO

I don't know.

IAGO

Is that possible?

CASSIO

I remember a jumble of impressions, but nothing distinctly. I remember a fight, but not why we were fighting. Oh God, why do men drink and lose their minds? Why do we party until we're like animals?

IAGO

Why, but you are now well enough. How came you thus
280   recovered?

CASSIO

It hath pleased the devil drunkenness to give place to the
devil wrath. One unperfectness shows me another, to
make me frankly despise myself.

IAGO

Come, you are too severe a moraler. As the time, the place,
285   and the condition of this country stands, I could heartily
wish this had not befallen. But since it is as it is, mend it
for your own good.

CASSIO

I will ask him for my place again, he shall tell me I am a
drunkard. Had I as many mouths as Hydra, such an
290   answer would stop them all. To be now a sensible man, by
and by a fool, and presently a beast! Oh, strange! Every
inordinate cup is unblessed and the ingredient is a devil.

IAGO

Come, come, good wine is a good familiar creature, if it be
well used. Exclaim no more against it. And, good
295   lieutenant, I think you think I love you.

CASSIO

I have well approved it, sir. I drunk!

IAGO

You or any man living may be drunk at a time, man. I tell you
what you shall do. Our general's wife is now the general. I
may say so in this respect, for that he hath devoted and given
300.   up himself to the contemplation, mark, and denotement of
her parts and graces. Confess yourself freely to her,
importune her help to put you in your place again. She is of
so free, so kind, so apt, so blessed a disposition, she holds it
a vice in her goodness not to do more than she is requested.
305.   This broken joint between you and her husband entreat her
to splinter, and, my fortunes against any lay worth naming,
this crack of your love shall grow stronger than it was before.

IAGO

You seem all right now. How did you get better?

CASSIO

My drunkenness went away when anger took over. One weakness led to another, to make me hate myself.

IAGO

Come on, you're being too hard on yourself. I wish none of this had happened, given the situation here, and your rank. But since this has happened, you should fix it for your own good.

CASSIO

I'll ask him for my position back again, and he'll tell me I'm a drunk. Even if I had a whole bunch of mouths, I wouldn't be able to answer that. I was a reasonable man, then I became a fool, and finally a beast! Oh, how strange! Every glass of liquor is damned, and the devil's the main ingredient!

IAGO

Come on now, wine is good for you, if you know how to use it. Don't say anything bad about wine anymore. Lieutenant, I think you know I'm your friend.

CASSIO

I know that, sir. Imagine, me, a drunk!

IAGO

Any man can get drunk sometime. I'll tell you what to do. Othello's wife has a lot of influence now. He's completely devoted to her. Go open your heart to her. Ask her to help you get back your position. She is so generous, kind, and ready to help that she thinks it's wrong not to do everything she can, even more than she is asked to do. Ask her to help you heal the rift between her husband and you. I'd bet my lucky stars your problem will be forgotten, and your relationship will be stronger than ever.

CASSIO

You advise me well.

IAGO

I protest, in the sincerity of love and honest kindness.

CASSIO

310   I think it freely, and betimes in the morning I will beseech
        the virtuous Desdemona to undertake for me. I am
        desperate of my fortunes if they check me.

IAGO

You are in the right. Good night, lieutenant, I must to the
watch.

CASSIO

315   Good night, honest Iago.

Exit

IAGO

And what's he then that says I play the villain?
When this advice is free I give and honest,
Probal to thinking and indeed the course
To win the Moor again? For 'tis most easy
320   Th' inclining Desdemona to subdue
In any honest suit. She's framed as fruitful
As the free elements. And then for her
To win the Moor, were to renounce his baptism,
All seals and symbols of redeemèd sin,
325   His soul is so enfettered to her love,
That she may make, unmake, do what she list,
Even as her appetite shall play the god
With his weak function. How am I then a villain
To counsel Cassio to this parallel course,
330   Directly to his good? Divinity of hell!
When devils will the blackest sins put on
They do suggest at first with heavenly shows
As I do now. For whiles this honest fool
Plies Desdemona to repair his fortune
335   And she for him pleads strongly to the Moor,
I'll pour this pestilence into his ear:

CASSIO

That's good advice.

IAGO

I'm helping you because I like and respect you.

CASSIO

I believe it completely. Early in the morning I'll go visit Desdemona and plead my case. My situation is desperate.

IAGO

You're doing the right thing. Good night, lieutenant. I've got to go to the guard tower.

CASSIO

Good night, honest Iago.

CASSIO exits.

IAGO

Who can say I'm evil when my advice is so good? That's really the best way to win the Moor back again. It's easy to get Desdemona on your side. She's full of good intentions. And the Moor loves her so much he would renounce his Christianity to keep her happy. He's so enslaved by love that she can make him do whatever she wants. How am I evil to advise Cassio to do exactly what'll do him good? That's the kind of argument you'd expect from Satan! When devils are about to commit their biggest sins they put on their most heavenly faces, just like I'm doing now. And while this fool is begging Desdemona to help him, and while she's pleading his case to the Moor, I'll poison the Moor's ear against her, hinting that she's taking Cassio's side because of her lust for him. The more she

That she repeals him for her body's lust.
And by how much she strives to do him good
She shall undo her credit with the Moor.
340   So will I turn her virtue into pitch
And out of her own goodness make the net
That shall enmesh them all.

Enter RODERIGO

                                    How now, Roderigo!

RODERIGO
I do follow here in the chase not like a hound that hunts,
but one that fills up the cry. My money is almost spent, I
345   have been tonight exceedingly well cudgeled, and I think
the issue will be I shall have so much experience for my
pains. And so, with no money at all and a little more wit,
return again to Venice.

IAGO
How poor are they that have not patience!
350   What wound did ever heal but by degrees?
Thou know'st we work by wit and not by witchcraft,
And wit depends on dilatory time.
Does't not go well? Cassio hath beaten thee.
And thou, by that small hurt, hath cashiered Cassio.
355   Though other things grow fair against the sun,
Yet fruits that blossom first will first be ripe.
Content thyself awhile. In troth, 'tis morning.
Pleasure and action make the hours seem short.
Retire thee, go where thou art billeted.
360   Away, I say, thou shalt know more hereafter.
Nay, get thee gone.
                                    Exit RODERIGO

tries to help Cassio, the more she'll shake Othello's confidence in her. And that's how I'll turn her good intentions into a big trap to snag them all.

RODERIGO *enters.*

Hello, Roderigo!

RODERIGO
I'm totally worn out. My chase is too much for me. I've spent most of my money, and tonight I got beaten up. The upshot is that I've got a little more experience. So with no money, but a little more wisdom, I'm going back to Venice.

IAGO
You're a poor man if you're this impatient! If you get hurt, does your wound heal immediately? No, it heals gradually. We achieve things with our intelligence, not by magic, and intelligent planning takes time. Aren't things going well? Cassio's beaten you up, but with that tiny sacrifice on your part, you got Cassio discharged! If we're patient, we'll be rewarded with the fruits of our labors. My God, it's morning. All this excitement has made the time fly by. Go back to where you're staying and go to sleep. Go on, I'm telling you. You'll understand better later. Go.

RODERIGO *exits.*

                              Two things are to be done:
My wife must move for Cassio to her mistress.
I'll set her on.
Myself, the while, to draw the Moor apart
And bring him jump when he may Cassio find
Soliciting his wife. Ay, that's the way.
Dull not device by coldness and delay.

                                                      Exit

365

Now two things still need to be done. My wife has to help make Desdemona take Cassio's side. I'll put her on that. And I need to take the Moor aside right at the moment when Cassio's talking to Desdemona, so he'll see them together. Yes, that's the way I'll do it. Let's not ruin a brilliant plan by being slow to act.

IAGO *exits.*

ACT THREE
SCENE 1

Enter CASSIO *and* MUSICIANS

CASSIO
> Masters, play here, I will content your pains.
> Something that's brief, and bid "Good morrow, general."

They play. Enter CLOWN

CLOWN
> Why masters, have your instruments been in Naples, that
> they speak i' th' nose thus?

MUSICIAN
> 5   How, sir? How?

CLOWN
> Are these, I pray you, wind instruments?

MUSICIAN
> Ay, marry, are they, sir.

CLOWN
> Oh, thereby hangs a tail.

MUSICIAN
> Whereby hangs a tale, sir?

CLOWN
> 10   Marry sir, by many a wind instrument that I know. But,
> masters, here's money for you, and the general so likes
> your music that he desires you, for love's sake, to make no
> more noise with it.

MUSICIAN
> Well, sir, we will not.

ACT THREE
SCENE 1

CASSIO *enters with* MUSICIANS.

CASSIO

Musicians, start playing here. I'll pay you for your trouble. Play something short that will put the general in a good mood.

The MUSICIANS *play. The* CLOWN *enters.*

CLOWN

Your instruments all have a nasal twang. Have they been to Naples?

Naples was considered a likely place to contract syphilis, which eats away at the bridge of the nose.

MUSICIAN

Excuse me?

CLOWN

Are these wind instruments?

MUSICIAN

Yes, they are.

CLOWN

Oh, there's the problem.

MUSICIAN

What's the problem?

CLOWN

Anyone full of hot air is a problem. But here's some money. The general likes your music a lot, but he asks you to stop playing now.

MUSICIAN

Well, we'll stop, then.

CLOWN

15   If you have any music that may not be heard, to 't again. But,
as they say, to hear music the general does not greatly care.

MUSICIAN

We have none such, sir.

CLOWN

Then put up your pipes in your bag, for I'll away. Go,
vanish into air, away!

Exeunt MUSICIANS

CASSIO

20   Dost thou hear, my honest friend?

CLOWN

No, I hear not your honest friend, I hear you.

CASSIO

Prithee, keep up thy quillets. There's a poor piece of gold
for thee. If the gentlewoman that attends the general's
wife be stirring, tell her there's one Cassio entreats her a

25   little favour of speech. Wilt thou do this?

CLOWN

She is stirring, sir. If she will stir hither, I shall seem to
notify unto her.

Exit CLOWN

Enter IAGO

In happy time, Iago.

IAGO

You have not been abed, then?

CASSIO

Why, no. The day had broke
Before we parted. I have made bold, Iago,

30   To send in to your wife. My suit to her
Is that she will to virtuous Desdemona
Procure me some access.

CLOWN

If you've got any music that can't be heard, then play that. But as I said, the general isn't really in the mood to hear music now.

MUSICIAN

We don't have any music that can't be heard.

CLOWN

Then pack up your instruments and go away. Go!

The MUSICIANS *exit.*

CASSIO

Do you hear, my friend?

CLOWN

No, I don't hear your friend. I hear you.

CASSIO

Please don't play games. (CASSIO *gives* CLOWN *money).* There's a bit of gold for you. When the woman taking care of the general's wife wakes up, could you please tell her that Cassio asks to speak with her?

CLOWN

She's awake, sir. If she feels like coming over here, I'll give her your message.

The CLOWN *exits.*

IAGO *enters.*

Good to see you, Iago.

IAGO

You didn't go to sleep, then?

CASSIO

No. When I left you it was already morning. I've been bold, Iago. I've asked to talk to your wife. I'm going to ask her to let me talk to Desdemona.

IAGO
          I'll send her to you presently,
          And I'll devise a mean to draw the Moor
35   Out of the way, that your converse and business
          May be more free.

CASSIO
          I humbly thank you for't.

                                        Exit IAGO

          I never knew a Florentine more kind and honest.

          Enter EMILIA

EMILIA
          Good morrow, good Lieutenant. I am sorry
40   For your displeasure, but all will sure be well.
          The general and his wife are talking of it,
          And she speaks for you stoutly. The Moor replies
          That he you hurt is of great fame in Cyprus
          And great affinity, and that in wholesome wisdom
45   He might not but refuse you. But he protests he loves you
          And needs no other suitor but his likings
          To take the safest occasion by the front
          To bring you in again.

CASSIO
                                        Yet I beseech you,
          If you think fit, or that it may be done,
50   Give me advantage of some brief discourse
          With Desdemona alone.

EMILIA
                                        Pray you come in.
          I will bestow you where you shall have time
          To speak your bosom freely.

CASSIO
                                        I am much bound to you.
                                        Exeunt

IAGO

I'll send her out to you now. I'll think of a plan to get the Moor out of the way, so you can speak more openly.

CASSIO

I humbly thank you.

IAGO exits.

Even for a Florentine, I never knew someone so kind and honest.

The citizens of Florence (who included Machiavelli) were not known for kindness and honesty, but Michael Cassio seems unaware of Florence's bad reputation.

EMILIA enters.

EMILIA

Good morning, lieutenant. I'm sorry about what happened, but I'm sure everything will turn out all right. The general and his wife are talking about it now, and she's defending you strongly. The Moor says the man you hurt is very important in Cyprus, and that under the circumstances he has no choice but to refuse to reinstate you. But he says he still loves and respects you, and based on his own feelings alone he's looking for an opportunity to safely take you back.

CASSIO

Please find a way to give me some time alone with Desdemona, if you think that's all right.

EMILIA

Please come in. I'll take you to a place where you can speak freely.

CASSIO

Thank you very much.

They exit.

ACT 3, SCENE 2

Enter OTHELLO, IAGO, *and* GENTLEMEN

OTHELLO
These letters give, Iago, to the pilot,
And by him do my duties to the senate.
That done, I will be walking on the works,
Repair there to me.

IAGO

5   Well, my good lord, I'll do 't.

OTHELLO
This fortification, gentlemen, shall we see 't?

GENTLEMEN
We'll wait upon your lordship.

Exeunt

ACT 3, SCENE 2

OTHELLO, IAGO *and* GENTLEMEN *enter.*

OTHELLO

Iago, give these letters to the ship's captain who brought me here, and ask him to pay my respects to the Senate of Venice. Now that's done, I'm going to walk on the fortification walls. Look for me there when you come back.

IAGO

I will, my lord.

OTHELLO

Shall we go see this fortification, men?

GENTLEMEN

We're at your service, my lord.

They all exit.

ACT 3, SCENE 3

Enter DESDEMONA, CASSIO, *and* EMILIA

DESDEMONA

Be thou assured, good Cassio, I will do
All my abilities in thy behalf.

EMILIA

Good madam, do. I warrant it grieves my husband
As if the cause were his.

DESDEMONA

5   Oh, that's an honest fellow. Do not doubt, Cassio,
But I will have my lord and you again
As friendly as you were.

CASSIO

                                              Bounteous madam,
Whatever shall become of Michael Cassio,
He's never anything but your true servant.

DESDEMONA

10   I know 't, I thank you. You do love my lord.
You have known him long, and be you well assured
He shall in strangeness stand no farther off
Than in a polite distance.

CASSIO

                                              Ay, but, lady,
That policy may either last so long,
15   Or feed upon such nice and waterish diet,
Or breed itself so out of circumstances,
That, I being absent and my place supplied,
My general will forget my love and service.

DESDEMONA

Do not doubt that. Before Emilia here
20   I give thee warrant of thy place. Assure thee,
If I do vow a friendship, I'll perform it
To the last article. My lord shall never rest,
I'll watch him tame and talk him out of patience.

ACT 3, SCENE 3

DESDEMONA, CASSIO *and* EMILIA *enter.*

DESDEMONA

> I'll do everything I can for you, Cassio.

EMILIA

> Please do, madam. My husband's so upset about Cassio's problem you'd think it was his own.

DESDEMONA

> Your husband's such a good man. Don't worry, Cassio. I'm sure you and my husband will be as friendly as you were before.

CASSIO

> My dear beautiful lady, whatever happens to Michael Cassio, he'll always be your humble servant.

DESDEMONA

> I know that. Thank you. You're my husband's friend and you've known him a long time. I assure you the only reason he's keeping away from you now is political.

CASSIO

> Yes, my lady. But those political considerations might last such a long time that the general will forget my love and service, especially if I'm gone and someone else has my job.

DESDEMONA

> That'll never happen. Emilia here will be my witness: I promise you that you'll get your position back again. And if I promise to help someone, I do everything I can. My husband will never get a moment's rest, I'll keep him up at night talking about you until he runs

His bed shall seem a school, his board a shrift,
25 I'll intermingle everything he does
With Cassio's suit. Therefore be merry, Cassio,
For thy solicitor shall rather die
Than give thy cause away.

Enter OTHELLO *and* IAGO

EMILIA
                                    Madam, here comes my lord.

CASSIO
Madam, I'll take my leave.

DESDEMONA
                                    Why, stay and hear me speak.

CASSIO
30 Madam, not now. I am very ill at ease,
Unfit for mine own purposes.

DESDEMONA
Well, do your discretion.

                                            Exit CASSIO

IAGO
Ha! I like not that.

OTHELLO
What dost thou say?

IAGO
35 Nothing, my lord, or if—I know not what.

OTHELLO
Was not that Cassio parted from my wife?

IAGO
Cassio, my lord? No, sure, I cannot think it
That he would steal away so guilty-like
Seeing you coming.

OTHELLO
40 I do believe 'twas he.

out of patience. He will think that his bed has become a conference table for discussing your problem—he won't be able to get away from it. I'll bring up your name at every moment. So cheer up. I'm your advocate, and I'd rather die than give up on you.

OTHELLO *and* IAGO *enter.*

EMILIA

Madam, here comes your husband.

CASSIO

Madam, I'd better leave now.

DESDEMONA

Why not stay and hear me talk to him?

CASSIO

No, madam. I'm very uncomfortable, and that won't help my case.

DESDEMONA

Well, do whatever you think best.

CASSIO *exits.*

IAGO

Hey! I don't like that.

OTHELLO

What did you say?

IAGO

Nothing, my lord, or if I did—I don't know what.

OTHELLO

Wasn't that Cassio leaving my wife?

IAGO

Cassio, my lord? No, I don't think so. He wouldn't sneak away looking so guilty when he saw you coming.

OTHELLO

I really think it was him.

DESDEMONA

How now, my lord?
I have been talking with a suitor here,
A man that languishes in your displeasure.

OTHELLO

Who is 't you mean?

DESDEMONA

Why, your lieutenant, Cassio. Good my lord,
45   If I have any grace or power to move you
His present reconciliation take.
For if he be not one that truly loves you,
That errs in ignorance and not in cunning,
I have no judgment in an honest face.
50   I prithee, call him back.

OTHELLO

Went he hence now?

DESDEMONA

Ay, sooth, so humbled
That he hath left part of his grief with me
To suffer with him. Good love, call him back.

OTHELLO

55   Not now, sweet Desdemona. Some other time.

DESDEMONA

But shall 't be shortly?

OTHELLO

The sooner, sweet, for you.

DESDEMONA

Shall 't be tonight at supper?

OTHELLO

No, not tonight.

DESDEMONA

Tomorrow dinner, then?

OTHELLO

I shall not dine at home,
I meet the captains at the citadel.

DESDEMONA

What's this, my lord? I was talking to a petitioner here just now, someone who's suffering from your anger.

OTHELLO

Who do you mean?

DESDEMONA

Your lieutenant, Cassio. Oh, if I've got any influence over you at all, please patch things up with him. In my judgment, this man truly loves you, and his mistake was innocent rather than wicked. Please call him and tell him to come back here.

OTHELLO

Was that him just now?

DESDEMONA

Yes. He feels so bad and humble that I feel bad along with him. My love, call him back in here.

OTHELLO

Not now, my sweet Desdemona. Some other time.

DESDEMONA

But will it be soon?

OTHELLO

Very soon, because you want it.

DESDEMONA

Will it be tonight at supper?

OTHELLO

No, not tonight.

DESDEMONA

Then tomorrow at dinner?

OTHELLO

I won't be eating dinner at home. I'll be meeting the captains at the citadel.

DESDEMONA

60   Why, then, tomorrow night, or Tuesday morn.
        On Tuesday noon, or night, or Wednesday morn.
        I prithee name the time, but let it not
        Exceed three days. In faith, he's penitent,
        And yet his trespass, in our common reason
65   (Save that, they say, the wars must make example
        Out of her best) is not, almost, a fault
        T' incur a private check. When shall he come?
        Tell me, Othello. I wonder in my soul
        What you would ask me that I should deny
70   Or stand so mamm'ring on. What? Michael Cassio
        That came a-wooing with you, and so many a time,
        When I have spoke of you dispraisingly,
        Hath ta'en your part, to have so much to do
        To bring him in? Trust me, I could do much—

OTHELLO

75   Prithee, no more. Let him come when he will,
        I will deny thee nothing.

DESDEMONA

                                    Why, this is not a boon,
        'Tis as I should entreat you wear your gloves,
        Or feed on nourishing dishes, or keep you warm,
        Or sue to you to do a peculiar profit
80   To your own person. Nay, when I have a suit
        Wherein I mean to touch your love indeed
        It shall be full of poise and difficult weight
        And fearful to be granted.

OTHELLO

                                    I will deny thee nothing!
        Whereon I do beseech thee, grant me this,
85   To leave me but a little to myself.

DESDEMONA

        Shall I deny you? No. Farewell, my lord.

OTHELLO

        Farewell, my Desdemona. I'll come to thee straight.

DESDEMONA

Well then, tomorrow night, or Tuesday morning. Or Tuesday noon or at night, or Wednesday morning. Please just name a time, but don't wait more than three days. He's very sorry. His mistake was hardly worth punishing him for in the first place—though in wartime it is sometimes necessary to make examples out of even the best soldiers. So when should he come? Tell me, Othello. I can't imagine you asking me for something and me telling you no or standing there muttering. Michael Cassio came with you when you were trying to win my love. Sometimes I'd criticize you to him, and he'd defend you. And now I have to make this big fuss about bringing him back? I swear, I could do so much—

OTHELLO

Please, no more. He can come whenever he wants. I won't refuse you anything.

DESDEMONA

Don't act like you're doing me a favor! This is like if I asked you to wear your gloves when it's cold outside, or eat nutritious food, or do something that's good for you. If I ever have to ask you for something that will put your luck to the test, it'll be something difficult and terrible.

OTHELLO

I won't deny you anything! But in return, please, do one thing for me: leave me alone for a little while.

DESDEMONA

Would I ever deny you anything? No. Goodbye, my husband.

OTHELLO

Goodbye, my Desdemona. I'll come see you right away.

DESDEMONA
Emilia, come.—Be as your fancies teach you.
Whate'er you be, I am obedient.

Exeunt DESDEMONA *and* EMILIA

OTHELLO
90   Excellent wretch! Perdition catch my soul
But I do love thee! And when I love thee not
Chaos is come again.

IAGO
My noble lord—

OTHELLO
What dost thou say, Iago?

IAGO
95   Did Michael Cassio, when you wooed my lady,
Know of your love?

OTHELLO
He did, from first to last.
Why dost thou ask?

IAGO
But for a satisfaction of my thought,
100   No further harm.

OTHELLO
Why of thy thought, Iago?

IAGO
I did not think he had been acquainted with her.

OTHELLO
Oh, yes, and went between us very oft.

IAGO
Indeed?

OTHELLO
Indeed? Ay, indeed! Discern'st thou aught in that?
105   Is he not honest?

IAGO
Honest, my lord?

DESDEMONA

Come here, Emilia.—Do whatever you feel like doing, my husband, and I'll obey you.

DESDEMONA and EMILIA exit.

OTHELLO

What a wonderful girl! God help me, I love you! And when I stop loving you, the universe will fall back into the chaos that was there when time began.

IAGO

My noble lord—

OTHELLO

What is it, Iago?

IAGO

When you were wooing Desdemona, did Michael Cassio know about it?

OTHELLO

Yes, he knew about it the whole time. Why do you ask?

IAGO

I was just curious. No reason.

OTHELLO

Why are you curious, Iago?

IAGO

I didn't realize he knew her.

OTHELLO

Oh, yes. He carried messages back and forth between us very often.

IAGO

Oh, really?

OTHELLO

Oh, really? Yes, really. Do you see something wrong with that? Isn't he an honest man?

IAGO

Honest, my lord?

OTHELLO
Honest, ay, honest.

IAGO
My lord, for aught I know.

OTHELLO
                              What dost thou think?

IAGO
Think, my lord?

OTHELLO
110   "Think, my lord?" Alas, thou echo'st me
As if there were some monster in thy thought
Too hideous to be shown. Thou dost mean something.
I heard thee say even now thou lik'st not that
When Cassio left my wife. What didst not like?
115   And when I told thee he was of my counsel
Of my whole course of wooing, thou cried'st "Indeed?"
And didst contract and purse thy brow together
As if thou then hadst shut up in thy brain
Some horrible conceit. If thou dost love me
120   Show me thy thought.

IAGO
My lord, you know I love you.

OTHELLO
I think thou dost.
And for I know thou 'rt full of love and honesty
And weigh'st thy words before thou giv'st them breath,
125   Therefore these stops of thine fright me the more.
For such things in a false disloyal knave
Are tricks of custom, but in a man that's just
They are close dilations, working from the heart,
That passion cannot rule.

IAGO
                              For Michael Cassio,
130   I dare be sworn, I think, that he is honest.

OTHELLO
I think so too.

OTHELLO

Honest, yes, honest.

IAGO

As far as I know, sir.

OTHELLO

What are you thinking?

IAGO

Thinking, my lord?

OTHELLO

"Thinking, my lord?" My God, you keep repeating everything I say as if you were thinking something too horrible to say out loud. You're thinking something. Just a minute ago I heard you say you didn't like it when Cassio left my wife. What didn't you like? And when I told you he was involved the whole time I was trying to get Desdemona, you were like, "Oh, really?" And then you frowned and wrinkled up your forehead as if you were imagining something horrible. If you're my friend, tell me what you're thinking.

IAGO

My lord, you know I'm your friend.

OTHELLO

I think you are. And I know you're full of love and honesty, and you think carefully before you speak. That's why these pauses of yours frighten me. If some fool were withholding things from me, I wouldn't think twice about it. If some lying, cheating villain acted like that, it would just be a trick. But when an honest man acts like that, you know he's wrestling with bad thoughts and can't help it.

IAGO

As for Michael Cassio, I think it would be safe for me to swear that he's honest.

OTHELLO

I think so too.

IAGO

                Men should be what they seem,
Or those that be not, would they might seem none!

OTHELLO

Certain, men should be what they seem.

IAGO

Why then I think Cassio's an honest man.

OTHELLO

135   Nay, yet there's more in this.
I prithee speak to me as to thy thinkings,
As thou dost ruminate, and give thy worst of thoughts
The worst of words.

IAGO

               Good my lord, pardon me,
Though I am bound to every act of duty
140   I am not bound to that all slaves are free to.
Utter my thoughts? Why, say they are vile and false,
As where's that palace whereinto foul things
Sometimes intrude not? Who has that breast so pure
Wherein uncleanly apprehensions
145   Keep leets and law-days and in sessions sit
With meditations lawful?

OTHELLO

Thou dost conspire against thy friend, Iago,
If thou but think'st him wronged and mak'st his ear
A stranger to thy thoughts.

IAGO

                  I do beseech you,
150   Though I perchance am vicious in my guess,
As, I confess, it is my nature's plague
To spy into abuses, and oft my jealousy
Shapes faults that are not, that your wisdom,
From one that so imperfectly conceits,
155   Would take no notice, nor build yourself a trouble
Out of his scattering and unsure observance.
It were not for your quiet nor your good,

IAGO

> People should be what they appear to be. If they're not honest, they shouldn't look like they are!

OTHELLO

> Absolutely, people should be what they appear to be.

IAGO

> In that case, I think Cassio's an honest man.

OTHELLO

> No, I think there's more to this than you're letting on. Please tell me what you're thinking—even your worst suspicions.

IAGO

> Please don't make me do that, sir. I have to obey all your orders, but surely I'm not obligated to reveal my deepest thoughts—even slaves aren't expected to do that. You want me to say what I'm thinking? What if my thoughts are disgusting and wrong? Even good people think horrible things sometimes. Who is so pure that they never think a bad thought?

OTHELLO

> You're not being a good friend, Iago, if you even *think* your friend has been wronged and you don't tell him about it.

IAGO

> Please don't ask me to tell you. I might be completely wrong. I have a bad tendency to be suspicious of people and to look too closely into what they're doing. Often I imagine crimes that aren't really there. You would be wise to ignore my weak guesses and imaginary suspicions, and don't worry yourself about the meaningless things I've noticed. For me to tell you my thoughts would only destroy your peace of mind, and

Nor for my manhood, honesty, and wisdom
To let you know my thoughts.

OTHELLO

What dost thou mean?

IAGO

160 Good name in man and woman, dear my lord,
Is the immediate jewel of their souls.
Who steals my purse steals trash. 'Tis something, nothing:
'Twas mine, 'tis his, and has been slave to thousands.
But he that filches from me my good name
165 Robs me of that which not enriches him
And makes me poor indeed.

OTHELLO

I'll know thy thoughts.

IAGO

You cannot, if my heart were in your hand,
Nor shall not, whilst 'tis in my custody.

OTHELLO
Ha!

IAGO

Oh, beware, my lord, of jealousy!
170 It is the green-eyed monster which doth mock
The meat it feeds on. That cuckold lives in bliss
Who, certain of his fate, loves not his wronger,
But, oh, what damnèd minutes tells he o'er
Who dotes, yet doubts— suspects, yet soundly loves!

OTHELLO
175 Oh, misery!

IAGO

Poor and content is rich, and rich enough,
But riches fineless is as poor as winter
To him that ever fears he shall be poor.
Good heaven, the souls of all my tribe defend
180 From jealousy!

it wouldn't be wise, honest, or responsible for me to tell them.

OTHELLO

What are you talking about?

IAGO

A good reputation is the most valuable thing we have—men and women alike. If you steal my money, you're just stealing trash. It's something, it's nothing: it's yours, it's mine, and it'll belong to thousands more. But if you steal my reputation, you're robbing me of something that doesn't make you richer, but makes me much poorer.

OTHELLO

I'm going to find out what you're thinking.

IAGO

You can't find that out, even if you held my heart in your hand you couldn't make me tell you. And as long my heart's inside my body, you never will.

OTHELLO

What?

IAGO

Beware of jealousy, my lord! It's a green-eyed monster that makes fun of the victims it devours. The man who knows his wife is cheating on him is happy, because at least he isn't friends with the man she's sleeping with. But think of the unhappiness of a man who worships his wife, yet doubts her faithfulness. He suspects her, but still loves her.

OTHELLO

Oh, what misery!

IAGO

The person who's poor and contented is rich enough. But infinite riches are nothing to someone who's always afraid he'll be poor. God, help us not be jealous!

OTHELLO
Why, why is this?
Think'st thou I'd make a life of jealousy,
To follow still the changes of the moon
With fresh suspicions? No! To be once in doubt
Is to be resolved. Exchange me for a goat
185 When I shall turn the business of my soul
To such exsufflicate and blowed surmises,
Matching thy inference. 'Tis not to make me jealous
To say my wife is fair, feeds well, loves company,
Is free of speech, sings, plays, and dances.
190 Where virtue is, these are more virtuous.
Nor from mine own weak merits will I draw
The smallest fear or doubt of her revolt,
For she had eyes and chose me. No, Iago,
I'll see before I doubt, when I doubt, prove,
195 And on the proof there is no more but this:
Away at once with love or jealousy!

IAGO
I am glad of this, for now I shall have reason
To show the love and duty that I bear you
With franker spirit. Therefore, as I am bound,
200 Receive it from me. I speak not yet of proof.
Look to your wife, observe her well with Cassio.
Wear your eyes thus, not jealous nor secure.
I would not have your free and noble nature
Out of self-bounty be abused. Look to 't.
205 I know our country disposition well.
In Venice they do let God see the pranks
They dare not show their husbands. Their best conscience
Is not to leave 't undone, but keep 't unknown.

OTHELLO
Dost thou say so?

OTHELLO

Why are you telling me this? Do you think I would live a life of jealousy, tormented by new suspicions every hour? No. If there's any doubt, there is no doubt. I might as well be a goat if I ever let myself become obsessed with the kind of suspicions you're implying. If you say my wife is beautiful, eats well, loves good company, speaks freely, sings, plays music, and dances well, you're not making me jealous. When a woman is virtuous, talents like these just make her better. And I'm not going to start feeling inferior. She had her eyes wide open when she chose me. No, Iago, I'll have to see some real evidence before I start suspecting her of anything bad, and when I suspect her, I'll look for proof, and if there's proof, that's when I'll let go of my love and my jealousy.

IAGO

I'm glad to hear you say that. Now I can show you my devotion and my duty with more honesty. So please listen to me. I'm not talking about proof yet. Watch your wife. Watch how she is with Cassio. Just watch— don't be either completely suspicious or completely trustful. I wouldn't want to see you taken advantage of because you're such an open and trusting guy. Watch out! I know the people of Venice well. They let God see things they wouldn't show their husbands. They don't avoid doing things that are wrong, they just try not to get caught.

OTHELLO

Do you really think so?

IAGO

210   She did deceive her father, marrying you,
       And when she seemed to shake and fear your looks,
       She loved them most.

OTHELLO

                                   And so she did.

IAGO

                                                    Why, go to then.
       She that, so young, could give out such a seeming,
       To seel her father's eyes up close as oak,
215   He thought 'twas witchcraft. But I am much to blame.
       I humbly do beseech you of your pardon
       For too much loving you.

OTHELLO

                                   I am bound to thee forever.

IAGO

       I see this hath a little dashed your spirits.

OTHELLO

       Not a jot, not a jot.

IAGO

                                   Trust me, I fear it has.
220   I hope you will consider what is spoke
       Comes from my love. But I do see you're moved.
       I am to pray you not to strain my speech
       To grosser issues nor to larger reach
       Than to suspicion.

OTHELLO

225   I will not.

IAGO

       Should you do so, my lord,
       My speech should fall into such vile success
       Which my thoughts aimed not at. Cassio's my worthy
                   friend—
       My lord, I see you're moved.

IAGO

She lied to her father to marry you. And when she pretended to be afraid of you, she loved you the most.

OTHELLO

That's right, she did.

IAGO

Well, there you go. She was so young, but she deceived her father so thoroughly he thought it was witchcraft! But I'm sorry I've blurted all this out. I beg your pardon for loving you too much.

OTHELLO

I'm indebted to you forever.

IAGO

You seem a little depressed about this.

OTHELLO

Not at all, not at all.

IAGO

Really, I'm afraid you are. I hope you remember that I said all this because I love you. But I see you're troubled. Please don't take what I said more seriously than it deserves to be taken.

OTHELLO

I won't.

IAGO

If you take it too seriously, it'll have bad effects that I didn't want it to have. Cassio's a good friend of mine—My lord, I can see you're upset.

OTHELLO

No, not much moved.

230   I do not think but Desdemona's honest.

IAGO

Long live she so. And long live you to think so.

OTHELLO

And yet how nature, erring from itself—

IAGO

Ay, there's the point. As, to be bold with you,
Not to affect many proposèd matches
235   Of her own clime, complexion, and degree,
Whereto we see in all things nature tends—
Foh! One may smell in such a will most rank,
Foul disproportions, thoughts unnatural.
But—pardon me—I do not in position
240   Distinctly speak of her, though I may fear
Her will, recoiling to her better judgment,
May fall to match you with her country forms,
And happily repent.

OTHELLO

Farewell, farewell.
If more thou dost perceive, let me know more.
245   Set on thy wife to observe. Leave me, Iago.

IAGO

My lord, I take my leave. *(going)*

OTHELLO

(aside) Why did I marry? This honest creature doubtless
Sees and knows more, much more, than he unfolds.

IAGO

(returns) My lord, I would I might entreat your honor
250   To scan this thing no farther. Leave it to time.
Although 'tis fit that Cassio have his place,
For sure, he fills it up with great ability,
Yet, if you please to hold him off awhile,
You shall by that perceive him and his means.
255   Note if your lady strain his entertainment

OTHELLO

No, not too upset. I'm sure Desdemona would never cheat on me.

IAGO

I hope she never does! And I hope you keep on thinking she wouldn't.

OTHELLO

But still, it's true that good things can go bad, away from their true natures—

IAGO

That's the point I'm trying to make. If I can be frank with you, she veered away from her own nature in turning down all those young men from her own country, with her skin color, with her status—everything her nature would have drawn her to—Ugh! You can almost smell the dark and ugly desires inside her, the unnatural thoughts—But—I'm sorry—I didn't mean to refer to her specifically just now. I only worry that she might snap back to her natural taste in men one day, and compare you unfavorably to other Italians.

OTHELLO

Goodbye, goodbye. If you see anything else, let me know. Tell your wife to watch her. Leave me alone now, Iago.

IAGO

My lord, I'll say goodbye now. *(beginning to exit)*

OTHELLO

(to himself) Why did I ever get married? I'm sure this good and honest man sees and knows more, much more, than he's telling me.

IAGO

(returning) My lord, please don't think about this any more. Time will tell. It's right for Cassio to have his lieutenancy back—he's very talented. But keep him away for a while, and you'll see how he goes about getting it back. Notice whether your wife insists on your

With any strong or vehement importunity.
Much will be seen in that. In the meantime,
Let me be thought too busy in my fears—
As worthy cause I have to fear I am—
260   And hold her free, I do beseech your honor.

OTHELLO
Fear not my government.

IAGO
                                    I once more take my leave.

                                                                Exit
OTHELLO
This fellow's of exceeding honesty
And knows all quantities, with a learnèd spirit,
Of human dealings. If I do prove her haggard,
265   Though that her jesses were my dear heartstrings,
I'd whistle her off and let her down the wind
To prey at fortune. Haply, for I am black
And have not those soft parts of conversation
That chamberers have, or for I am declined
270   Into the vale of years—yet that's not much—
She's gone, I am abused, and my relief
Must be to loathe her. Oh, curse of marriage
That we can call these delicate creatures ours
And not their appetites! I had rather be a toad
275   And live upon the vapor of a dungeon
Than keep a corner in the thing I love
For others' uses. Yet 'tis the plague to great ones,
Prerogatived are they less than the base.
'Tis destiny unshunnable, like death.
280   Even then this forkèd plague is fated to us
When we do quicken. Look where she comes.

Enter DESDEMONA *and* EMILIA

If she be false, heaven mocked itself.
I'll not believe 't.

giving it back to him. That will tell you a lot. But in the meantime, just assume that I'm paranoid—as I'm pretty sure I am—and keep thinking she's innocent, please.

OTHELLO

Don't worry about how I handle it.

IAGO

I'll say goodbye once more.

IAGO exits.

OTHELLO

This Iago is extremely honest and good, and he knows a lot about human behavior. If it turns out that she really is running around on me, I'll send her away, even though it'll break my heart. Maybe because I'm black, and I don't have nice manners like courtiers do, or because I'm getting old—but that's not much— She's gone, and I've been cheated on. I have no choice but to hate her. Oh what a curse marriage is! We think our beautiful wives belong to us, but their desires are free! I'd rather be a toad in a moldy basement than to have only a part of someone I love, sharing the rest of her with others. This is the plague of important men—our wives betray us more than those of poor men. It's our destiny, like death. We are destined to be betrayed when we are born. Oh, here she comes.

DESDEMONA *and* EMILIA *enter.*

If she's cheated on me, then heaven itself is a fake. I don't believe it.

DESDEMONA

How now, my dear Othello?
Your dinner, and the generous islanders
285   By you invited, do attend your presence.

OTHELLO

I am to blame.

DESDEMONA

Why do you speak so faintly?
Are you not well?

OTHELLO

I have a pain upon my forehead, here.

DESDEMONA

290   Why that's with watching, 'twill away again.
Let me but bind it hard, within this hour
It will be well. *(pulls out a handkerchief)*

OTHELLO

Your napkin is too little,
Let it alone.

Her handkerchief drops

295   Come, I'll go in with you.

DESDEMONA

I am very sorry that you are not well.

Exeunt OTHELLO *and* DESDEMONA

EMILIA

(picks up the handkercheif)
I am glad I have found this napkin,
This was her first remembrance from the Moor.
My wayward husband hath a hundred times

DESDEMONA

What's going on, Othello, darling? The nobles of Cyprus whom you invited to dinner are waiting for you.

OTHELLO

I'm sorry.

DESDEMONA

Why are you whispering? Are you sick?

OTHELLO

I have a headache, right here in my forehead.

In Shakespeare's day, cuckolds, or men whose wives cheated on them, were imagined to have horns growing from their heads. Othello is alluding to this.

DESDEMONA

That's from lack of sleep. It'll go away. Let me wrap up your head, and it will feel okay in less than an hour. *(she pulls out a handkerchief)*

OTHELLO

No, your handkerchief's too little. Leave my head alone.

The handkerchief falls to the floor.

Come on, I'll escort you to dinner.

DESDEMONA

I'm very sorry you're not feeling well.

OTHELLO *and* DESDEMONA *exit.*

EMILIA

(picking up the handkerchief) I'm glad I found this handkerchief. It's the first keepsake the Moor gave her. My stubborn husband has asked me to steal it a

300 Wooed me to steal it, but she so loves the token
(For he conjured her she should ever keep it)
That she reserves it evermore about her
To kiss and talk to. I'll have the work ta'en out
And give 't Iago. What he will do with it
305 Heaven knows, not I.
I nothing but to please his fantasy.

Enter IAGO

IAGO
How now! What do you here alone?

EMILIA
Do not you chide. I have a thing for you.

IAGO
A thing for me? It is a common thing—

EMILIA
310 Ha?

IAGO
To have a foolish wife.

EMILIA
Oh, is that all? What will you give me now
For the same handkerchief?

IAGO
What handkerchief?

EMILIA
315 What handkerchief?
Why, that the Moor first gave to Desdemona,
That which so often you did bid me steal.

IAGO
Hast stolen it from her?

EMILIA
No, but she let it drop by negligence
320 And, to th' advantage, I being here, took 't up.
Look, here it is.

hundred times. But she loves it so much (since Othello told her she should always keep it with her) that she always keeps it near her to kiss it and talk to it. I'll copy the embroidery pattern and then give it to Iago. Heaven knows what he's going to do with it. I only try to satisfy his whims.

IAGO *enters.*

IAGO

What's going on? What are you doing here alone?

EMILIA

Don't snap at me. I've got something for you.

IAGO

You've got something for me? It's a common thing—

"Thing" was slang for vagina. By saying that Emilia's "thing" is "common," Iago implies that she lets anyone have sex with her

EMILIA

What?

IAGO

—to have a stupid wife.

EMILIA

Oh, is that so? And what would you give me for the handkerchief?

IAGO

What handkerchief?

EMILIA

What handkerchief? The one the Moor gave to Desdemona, which you asked me to steal so many times.

IAGO

You stole it from her?

EMILIA

No, actually. She dropped it carelessly, and, seizing the opportunity, since I was here, I picked it up. Look, here it is.

IAGO

A good wench, give it me.

EMILIA

What will you do with 't, that you have been so earnest
To have me filch it?

IAGO

Why, what is that to you?

EMILIA

If it be not for some purpose of import,
325   Give 't me again. Poor lady, she'll run mad
When she shall lack it.

IAGO

Be not acknown on 't,
I have use for it. Go, leave me.

Exit EMILIA

I will in Cassio's lodging lose this napkin
330   And let him find it. Trifles light as air
Are to the jealous confirmations strong
As proofs of holy writ. This may do something.
The Moor already changes with my poison.
Dangerous conceits are in their natures poisons
335   Which at the first are scarce found to distaste,
But with a little act upon the blood
Burn like the mines of sulfur.

Enter OTHELLO

I did say so.
Look, where he comes. Not poppy nor mandragora
Nor all the drowsy syrups of the world,
340   Shall ever medicine thee to that sweet sleep
Which thou owedst yesterday.

OTHELLO

Ha! Ha! False to me?

IAGO

Why, how now, general? No more of that.

IAGO

Good girl, give it to me.

EMILIA

And what are you going to do with it? Why did you want it so much that you begged me to steal it?

IAGO

What's it to you?

EMILIA

If you don't need it for some important reason, then give it back to me. Poor lady, she'll go crazy when she sees it's missing.

IAGO

Don't admit to knowing anything about it. I need it. Now go, leave me.

EMILIA exits.

I'll leave this handkerchief at Cassio's house and let him find it. To a jealous man, a meaningless little thing like this looks like absolute proof. This handkerchief may be useful to me. The Moor's mind has already become infected with my poisonous suggestions. Ideas can be like poisons. At first they hardly even taste bad, but once they get into your blood they start burning like hot lava.

OTHELLO enters.

Here he comes. No drugs or sleeping pills will ever give you the restful sleep that you had last night.

OTHELLO

Argh! She's cheating on me?

IAGO

Oh, general, please, no more of that!

OTHELLO
    Avaunt! Be gone! Thou hast set me on the rack.
    I swear 'tis better to be much abused
345   Than but to know 't a little.

IAGO
                    How now, my lord!

OTHELLO
    What sense had I in her stol'n hours of lust?
    I saw 't not, thought it not, it harmed not me.
    I slept the next night well, fed well, was free and merry.
    I found not Cassio's kisses on her lips.
350   He that is robbed, not wanting what is stol'n,
    Let him not know't, and he's not robbed at all.

IAGO
    I am sorry to hear this.

OTHELLO
    I had been happy if the general camp,
    Pioneers and all, had tasted her sweet body,
355   So I had nothing known. Oh, now forever
    Farewell the tranquil mind! Farewell content!
    Farewell the plumèd troops and the big wars
    That makes ambition virtue! Oh, farewell!
    Farewell the neighing steed and the shrill trump,
360   The spirit-stirring drum, th' ear-piercing fife,
    The royal banner, and all quality,
    Pride, pomp, and circumstance of glorious war!
    And O you mortal engines, whose rude throats
    The immortal Jove's dead clamors counterfeit,
365   Farewell! Othello's occupation's gone.

IAGO
    Is 't possible, my lord?

OTHELLO
    Villain, be sure thou prove my love a whore,
    Be sure of it. Give me the ocular proof
    Or by the worth of mine eternal soul
370   Thou hadst been better have been born a dog
    Than answer my waked wrath!

OTHELLO

Get lost! You've tortured me with these thoughts. It is better to be tricked completely than to only suspect a little.

IAGO

What's with you, my lord?

OTHELLO

I had no idea she was cheating on me. I never saw it or suspected it, so it never hurt me. I slept well, ate well, and was happy. I never saw Cassio's kisses on her lips. A man who's robbed, but doesn't miss what's stolen, isn't robbed at all.

IAGO

I'm sorry to hear this.

OTHELLO

I would've been happy if the whole army had had sex with her, the lowest-ranking grunts and all, as long as I didn't know anything about it. Oh, goodbye to my peace of mind! Goodbye to my happiness! Goodbye to the soldiers and to the wars that make men great! Goodbye! Goodbye to the horses and the trumpets and the drums, the flute and the splendid banners, and all those proud displays and pageantry of war! And you deadly cannons that roar like thunderbolts thrown by the gods, goodbye! Othello's career is over.

IAGO

Is this possible, my lord?

OTHELLO

You villain, you'd better be able to prove my wife's a whore! Be sure of it. Get me proof I can see. If you can't, trust me, you won't want to feel my rage!

IAGO

Is 't come to this?

OTHELLO

Make me to see 't, or at the least so prove it
That the probation bear no hinge nor loop
To hang a doubt on, or woe upon thy life!

IAGO

375   My noble lord—

OTHELLO

If thou dost slander her and torture me,
Never pray more. Abandon all remorse.
On horror's head horrors accumulate,
Do deeds to make heaven weep, all earth amazed,
380   For nothing canst thou to damnation add
Greater than that.

IAGO

Oh, grace! Oh, heaven forgive me!
Are you a man? Have you a soul or sense?
God buy you, take mine office. O wretched fool
That lov'st to make thine honesty a vice!
385   O monstrous world! Take note, take note, O world,
To be direct and honest is not safe.
I thank you for this profit, and from hence
I'll love no friend, sith love breeds such offence.

OTHELLO

Nay, stay. Thou shouldst be honest.

IAGO

390   I should be wise, for honesty's a fool
And loses that it works for.

OTHELLO

By the world,
I think my wife be honest and think she is not.
I think that thou art just and think thou art not.
I'll have some proof. Her name, that was as fresh
395   As Dian's visage, is now begrimed and black
As mine own face. If there be cords or knives,

IAGO

Has it come to this?

OTHELLO

Show me, or at least prove it beyond the shadow of a doubt. If you can't, your life is worthless!

IAGO

My noble lord—

OTHELLO

If you're slandering her just to torture me, then it'll be no use to pray for mercy or say you're sorry. You might as well go ahead and commit every unspeakable crime you can think of, because there's nothing you could that would top what you've already done!

IAGO

Oh, heaven help me! Aren't you a rational human being? Don't you have any sense at all? Goodbye. I resign my official position. I'm such an idiot for always telling the truth! What a horrible world we live in! Listen, pay attention, everybody. It's not safe to be straightforward and honest. I'm glad you've taught me this valuable lesson. From now on, I'll never try to help a friend when it hurts him so much to hear the truth.

OTHELLO

No, stop. You should always be honest.

IAGO

I should always be wise. Honesty's stupid, it makes me lose my friends even when I'm trying to help them.

OTHELLO

By referring to instruments of death, Othello implies that he wants to commit either suicide or murder

I swear, I think my wife's faithful, and I think she's not. I think you're trustworthy one minute and then not the next. I need proof! Her reputation was as pure as the snow, but now it's as dirty and black as my own face. As long as there are ropes, knives, poison, fire, or

Poison, or fire, or suffocating streams,
I'll not endure it. Would I were satisfied!

IAGO

I see, sir, you are eaten up with passion.
I do repent me that I put it to you.
You would be satisfied?

OTHELLO

Would? Nay, and I will.

IAGO

And may, but how? How satisfied, my lord?
Would you, the supervisor, grossly gape on,
Behold her topped?

OTHELLO

Death and damnation! Oh!

IAGO

It were a tedious difficulty, I think,
To bring them to that prospect. Damn them then,
If ever mortal eyes do see them bolster
More than their own! What then? How then?
What shall I say? Where's satisfaction?
It is impossible you should see this,
Were they as prime as goats, as hot as monkeys,
As salt as wolves in pride, and fools as gross
As ignorance made drunk. But yet, I say,
If imputation and strong circumstances
Which lead directly to the door of truth
Will give you satisfaction, you may have 't.

OTHELLO

Give me a living reason she's disloyal.

IAGO

I do not like the office.
But, sith I am entered in this cause so far,
Pricked to 't by foolish honesty and love,
I will go on. I lay with Cassio lately
And, being troubled with a raging tooth,
I could not sleep. There are a kind of men
So loose of soul that in their sleeps will mutter

streams to drown in, I won't stand for this. Oh, how I wish I knew the truth!

IAGO

I see you're all eaten up with emotion. I'm sorry I said anything. You want proof?

OTHELLO

Want? Yes, I want it, and I'll get it.

IAGO

But how? How will you get proof? Are you going to hide and watch them having sex?

OTHELLO

Death and damnation! Oh!

IAGO

I think it would be very hard to arrange for them to have sex while you watched. If anyone sees them in bed together besides themselves, I guess we could damn them then. So what can we do? What can I say? What proof is there? It'd be impossible for you to watch them, even if they were as horny as animals in heat and as stupid as drunks. But if you would be willing to accept circumstantial evidence as proof, we can get that.

OTHELLO

Give me one good reason to think she's cheating on me.

IAGO

I don't like what you're asking me to do. But since I've gotten myself involved this far, because I'm so stupidly honest and because I like you so much, I'll keep going. I recently shared a bed with Cassio, and I couldn't sleep because of a raging toothache. Well, some people talk in their sleep, and Cassio is one of

425   Their affairs. One of this kind is Cassio.
    In sleep I heard him say "Sweet Desdemona,
    Let us be wary, let us hide our loves."
    And then, sir, would he gripe and wring my hand,
    Cry "O sweet creature!" and then kiss me hard,
430   As if he plucked up kisses by the roots
    That grew upon my lips, lay his leg
    Over my thigh, and sigh, and kiss, and then
    Cry "Cursed fate that gave thee to the Moor!"

OTHELLO
    Oh, monstrous! Monstrous!

IAGO
435   Nay, this was but his dream.

OTHELLO
    But this denoted a foregone conclusion.

IAGO
    'Tis a shrewd doubt, though it be but a dream.
    And this may help to thicken other proofs
    That do demonstrate thinly.

OTHELLO
                        I'll tear her all to pieces!

IAGO
440   Nay, yet be wise, yet we see nothing done,
    She may be honest yet. Tell me but this,
    Have you not sometimes seen a handkerchief
    Spotted with strawberries in your wife's hand?

OTHELLO
    I gave her such a one, 'twas my first gift.

IAGO
445   I know not that, but such a handkerchief—
    I am sure it was your wife's—did I today
    See Cassio wipe his beard with.

OTHELLO
                        If it be that—

IAGO
    If it be that, or any that was hers,
    It speaks against her with the other proofs.

them. I heard him saying, "Sweet Desdemona, let's be careful and hide our love," in his sleep. And then he grabbed my hand and said, "Oh, my darling!" and kissed me hard, as if he were trying to suck my lips off. Then he put his leg over mine, and sighed and kissed me, and said, "Damn fate for giving you to the Moor!"

OTHELLO

Oh, that's monstrous! Monstrous!

IAGO

No, it was just a dream.

OTHELLO

But it shows that something has already happened.

IAGO

It's a reason for suspicion, even though it's just a dream. And it might back up other evidence that may seem too flimsy.

OTHELLO

I'll tear her to pieces!

IAGO

No, be reasonable. We don't have any proof yet. She might still be faithful. Just tell me this: have you ever seen her holding a handkerchief with an embroidered strawberry pattern on it?

OTHELLO

Yes, I gave her one like that. It was my first gift to her.

IAGO

I don't know about that, but I saw a handkerchief like that today. I'm sure it belongs to your wife, and I saw Cassio use it to wipe his beard.

OTHELLO

If it's the same one—

IAGO

If it's the same one, or any one that belongs to her, then together with the other evidence it's pretty strong.

OTHELLO

450   Oh, that the slave had forty thousand lives!
         One is too poor, too weak for my revenge.
         Now do I see 'tis true. Look here, Iago,
         All my fond love thus do I blow to heaven.
         'Tis gone.
455   Arise, black vengeance, from the hollow hell!
         Yield up, O love, thy crown and hearted throne
         To tyrannous hate! Swell, bosom, with thy fraught,
         For 'tis of aspics' tongues!

IAGO

                         Yet be content.

OTHELLO

         Oh, blood, blood, blood!

IAGO

                    Patience, I say. Your mind may change.

OTHELLO

460   Never, Iago. Like to the Pontic sea,
         Whose icy current and compulsive course
         Ne'er keeps retiring ebb but keeps due on
         To the Propontic and the Hellespont,
         Even so my bloody thoughts with violent pace
465   Shall ne'er look back, ne'er ebb to humble love
         Till that a capable and wide revenge
         Swallow them up. Now, by yon marble heaven,
         In the due reverence of a sacred vow
         I here engage my words. *(he kneels)*

IAGO

                       Do not rise yet.
470   Witness, you ever-burning lights above,
         You elements that clip us round about,
         Witness that here Iago doth give up
         The execution of his wit, hands, heart,
         To wronged Othello's service. Let him command,
475   And to obey shall be in me remorse,
         What bloody business ever.

OTHELLO

Oh, I'd kill that bastard Cassio forty thousand times if I could! Killing him once is not enough revenge. Now I see it's true. Oh, Iago, all the love I felt is gone, vanished in the wind. Welcome, hatred and vengeance! Get out of my heart, love! My heart feels like it's full of poisonous snakes!

IAGO

Calm down—

OTHELLO

I want blood!

IAGO

Be patient, I'm telling you. You may change your mind later.

OTHELLO

Never, Iago. My thoughts of revenge are flowing through me like a violent river, never turning back to love, only flowing toward full revenge that'll swallow them up. I swear to God I'll get revenge. *(he kneels)*

IAGO

Don't get up yet. Let heaven be my witness—I'm putting my mind, my heart, and my hands in Othello's control. Let him command me, and I'll do whatever he asks, no matter how violent.

OTHELLO
                                    I greet thy love
            Not with vain thanks but with acceptance bounteous,
            And will upon the instant put thee to 't.
            Within these three days let me hear thee say
480   That Cassio's not alive.

IAGO
                                    My friend is dead,
            'Tis done at your request. But let her live.

OTHELLO
            Damn her, lewd minx! Oh, damn her, damn her!
            Come, go with me apart. I will withdraw
            To furnish me with some swift means of death
485   For the fair devil. Now art thou my lieutenant.

IAGO
            I am your own for ever.

                                                    Exeunt

OTHELLO

I accept your devotion with my deepest love. I'll put you to the test right away. Within the next three days I want to hear you tell me that Cassio's dead.

IAGO

My friend Cassio is dead. It's done, because you request it. But let her live.

OTHELLO

Damn her, the wicked whore! Oh, damn her, damn her! Come away with me. I'm going inside to think up some way to kill that beautiful devil. You're my lieutenant now.

IAGO

I'm yours forever.

They exit.

ACT 3, SCENE 4

Enter DESDEMONA, EMILIA, *and* CLOWN

DESDEMONA
Do you know, sirrah, where Lieutenant Cassio lies?

CLOWN
I dare not say he lies anywhere.

DESDEMONA
Why, man?

CLOWN
He's a soldier, and for one to say a soldier lies, 'tis
5   stabbing.

DESDEMONA
Go to. Where lodges he?

CLOWN
To tell you where he lodges is to tell you where I lie.

DESDEMONA
Can anything be made of this?

CLOWN
I know not where he lodges, and for me to devise a lodging
10   and say he lies here, or he lies there, were to lie in mine own
throat.

DESDEMONA
Can you inquire him out and be edified by report?

CLOWN
I will catechize the world for him, that is, make questions,
and by them answer.

DESDEMONA
15   Seek him, bid him come hither. Tell him I have moved my
lord on his behalf, and hope all will be well.

CLOWN
To do this is within the compass of man's wit, and
therefore I will attempt the doing it.

Exit

ACT 3, SCENE 4

DESDEMONA, EMILIA *and the* CLOWN *enter.*

DESDEMONA

lies in = sleeps in →

Excuse me, do you know which room Lieutenant Cassio lies in?

CLOWN

I wouldn't dare say he lies anywhere.

DESDEMONA

Why do you say that?

CLOWN

He's a soldier. If I accused a soldier of lying, he'd stab me.

DESDEMONA

Oh, come on. Where does he sleep?

CLOWN

Telling you where he's sleeping is like telling you where I'm lying.

DESDEMONA

What on earth does that mean?

CLOWN

I don't know where he's staying, so if I told you he's sleeping here or there, I'd be lying.

DESDEMONA

Can you ask around and find out?

CLOWN

I'll go ask questions everywhere.

DESDEMONA

Find him and tell him to come here. Tell him I've spoken to my husband on his behalf, and I think everything will be all right.

CLOWN

I think I can do that. It's not too much to ask.

CLOWN *exits.*

DESDEMONA
Where should I lose that handkerchief, Emilia?

EMILIA

20   I know not, madam.

DESDEMONA
Believe me, I had rather have lost my purse
Full of crusadoes. And but my noble Moor
Is true of mind and made of no such baseness
As jealous creatures are, it were enough

25   To put him to ill thinking.

EMILIA
Is he not jealous?

DESDEMONA
Who, he? I think the sun where he was born
Drew all such humors from him.

EMILIA
Look where he comes.

Enter OTHELLO

DESDEMONA

30   I will not leave him now till Cassio
Be called to him.—How is 't with you, my lord?

OTHELLO
Well, my good lady.—*(aside)* Oh, hardness to dissemble!—
How do you, Desdemona?

DESDEMONA
                                        Well, my good lord.

OTHELLO
Give me your hand. This hand is moist, my lady.

DESDEMONA

35   It hath felt no age nor known no sorrow.

OTHELLO
This argues fruitfulness and liberal heart.
Hot, hot, and moist. This hand of yours requires
A sequester from liberty, fasting, and prayer,

DESDEMONA

Where could I have lost that handkerchief, Emilia?

EMILIA

I don't know, madam.

DESDEMONA

Believe me, I'd rather have lost a purse full of gold coins. This would be enough to make my husband suspect me, if he wasn't so free of jealousy.

EMILIA

He's not jealous?

DESDEMONA

Who, him? I think all tendencies to jealousy were burned out of him by the sun of his native land.

EMILIA

Look, here he comes.

OTHELLO *enters.*

DESDEMONA

I won't leave him alone until he gives Cassio his job back.—How are you, my lord?

OTHELLO

I'm fine, my lady.—*(to himself)* Oh, it's so hard to pretend!—How are you, Desdemona?

DESDEMONA

I'm fine, my lord.

OTHELLO

Give me your hand. Your hand's moist, my lady.

Moist hands were supposed to indicate a tendency toward love.

DESDEMONA

It's moist because it's still young and inexperienced.

OTHELLO

It says you're fertile, and you've got a giving heart. Hot, hot and moist. With a hand like this you need to

Much castigation, exercise devout,
40   For here's a young and sweating devil here,
That commonly rebels. 'Tis a good hand,
A frank one.

DESDEMONA
You may indeed say so,
For 'twas that hand that gave away my heart.

OTHELLO
A liberal hand. The hearts of old gave hands,
45   But our new heraldry is hands, not hearts.

DESDEMONA
I cannot speak of this. Come now, your promise.

OTHELLO
What promise, chuck?

DESDEMONA
I have sent to bid Cassio come speak with you.

OTHELLO
I have a salt and sorry rheum offends me.
50   Lend me thy handkerchief.

DESDEMONA
Here, my lord.

OTHELLO
That which I gave you.

DESDEMONA
I have it not about me.

OTHELLO
Not?

DESDEMONA
No, indeed, my lord.

OTHELLO
That's a fault. That handkerchief
Did an Egyptian to my mother give,
She was a charmer and could almost read

fast and pray to stave off temptations. Someone with a young sweating hand like this one is bound to act up sooner or later. It's a nice hand, an open one.

DESDEMONA

You're right to say that. This was the hand that gave you my heart.

OTHELLO

This hand gives itself away very freely. In the old days, people used to give their hearts to each other when they joined their hands in marriage. But these days, people give each other their hands without their hearts.

DESDEMONA

I don't know about that. Now, don't forget, you promised me something.

OTHELLO

What did I promise, my dear?

DESDEMONA

I sent for Cassio to come talk with you.

OTHELLO

I have a bad cold that's bothering me. Lend me your handkerchief.

DESDEMONA

Here, my lord.

OTHELLO

No, the one I gave you.

DESDEMONA

I don't have it with me.

OTHELLO

You don't?

DESDEMONA

No, my lord.

OTHELLO

That's not good. An Egyptian woman gave that handkerchief to my mother. She was a witch, and she could

55   The thoughts of people. She told her, while she kept it
      'Twould make her amiable and subdue my father
      Entirely to her love, but if she lost it
      Or made gift of it, my father's eye
      Should hold her loathèd and his spirits should hunt
60   After new fancies. She, dying, gave it me
      And bid me, when my fate would have me wived,
      To give it her. I did so, and take heed on 't,
      Make it a darling like your precious eye.
      To lose 't or give 't away were such perdition
65   As nothing else could match.

DESDEMONA

                                        Is 't possible?

OTHELLO
      'Tis true. There's magic in the web of it.
      A sibyl, that had numbered in the world
      The sun to course two hundred compasses,
      In her prophetic fury sewed the work.
70   The worms were hallowed that did breed the silk,
      And it was dyed in mummy which the skillful
      Conserved of maidens' hearts.

DESDEMONA

                                        Indeed? Is 't true?

OTHELLO
      Most veritable, therefore look to 't well.

DESDEMONA
      Then would to Heaven that I had never seen 't!

OTHELLO
75   Ha! Wherefore?

DESDEMONA
      Why do you speak so startingly and rash?

OTHELLO
      Is 't lost? Is 't gone? Speak, is 't out o' th' way?

DESDEMONA
      Bless us!

almost read people's thoughts. She told my mother
that as long as she kept it with her, my father would
love and desire her. But if she lost it or gave it away, my
father would start hating her and looking
at other women. When she was dying she gave it to me
and told me to give it to my wife when I got married.
I did. So pay attention. Treat it as something precious.
Losing it or giving it away would be an unspeakable
loss, a loss like none other.

DESDEMONA

Is that possible?

OTHELLO

Yes, it's true. There's magic in its fabric. A two-hun-
dred-year-old witch sewed it while she was in a
fevered trance. The silk came from sacred silkworms,
and it was dyed with fluid made from embalmed vir-
gins' hearts.

DESDEMONA

Really? Is that true?

OTHELLO

It's absolutely true, so take good care of it.

DESDEMONA

I wish I had never seen it!

OTHELLO

Ha! Why?

DESDEMONA

Why are you yelling at me so angrily?

OTHELLO

Is it lost? Is it gone? Tell me, is it missing?

DESDEMONA

God help me!

OTHELLO
Say you?

DESDEMONA
80 It is not lost, but what and if it were?

OTHELLO
How!

DESDEMONA
I say, it is not lost.

OTHELLO
Fetch 't, let me see 't.

DESDEMONA
Why, so I can, sir, but I will not now.
This is a trick to put me from my suit.
85 Pray you, let Cassio be received again.

OTHELLO
Fetch me the handkerchief—my mind misgives.

DESDEMONA
Come, come,
You'll never meet a more sufficient man.

OTHELLO
The handkerchief!

DESDEMONA
A man that all his time
90 Hath founded his good fortunes on your love,
Shared dangers with you—

OTHELLO
The handkerchief!

DESDEMONA
In sooth, you are to blame.

OTHELLO
Away!

Exit

EMILIA
95 Is not this man jealous?

OTHELLO

What do you have to say for yourself?

DESDEMONA

It's not lost, but what if it were?

OTHELLO

What do you mean?

DESDEMONA

I'm telling you, it's not lost.

OTHELLO

Then bring it here. Let me see it.

DESDEMONA

I could, sir. But I don't want to now. This is just a trick to take my mind off what I'm asking you for. Please hire Cassio again.

OTHELLO

Bring me the handkerchief—My mind is full of doubt.

DESDEMONA

Come on. You know you'll never find a more capable man.

OTHELLO

The handkerchief!

DESDEMONA

He's counted on your friendship for his success. He's shared dangers with you—

OTHELLO

The handkerchief!

DESDEMONA

Really, I don't think you're behaving very well.

OTHELLO

Damn it!

OTHELLO exits.

EMILIA

And you say he's not jealous?

DESDEMONA
                                        I ne'er saw this before.
Sure, there's some wonder in this handkerchief,
I am most unhappy in the loss of it.

EMILIA
'Tis not a year or two shows us a man.

They are all but stomachs, and we all but food.
100   To eat us hungerly, and when they are full,
They belch us. Look you, Cassio and my husband!

Enter CASSIO *and* IAGO

IAGO
There is no other way. 'Tis she must do 't,
And, lo, the happiness! Go and importune her.

DESDEMONA
How now, good Cassio, what's the news with you?

CASSIO
105   Madam, my former suit. I do beseech you
That by your virtuous means I may again
Exist, and be a member of his love
Whom I, with all the office of my heart
Entirely honor. I would not be delayed.
110   If my offence be of such mortal kind
That nor my service past, nor present sorrows,
Nor purposed merit in futurity,
Can ransom me into his love again,
But to know so must be my benefit.
115   So shall I clothe me in a forced content,
And shut myself up in some other course,
To fortune's alms.

DESDEMONA

> I never saw him like this before. There must be some magic in that handkerchief. I'm miserable that I lost it.

EMILIA

> Men are all the same, but it takes longer than a year or two to see how bad they are. They're like stomachs and we're just the food. They eat us up hungrily, and when they're full, they vomit us up. Look, here comes Cassio and my husband.

IAGO and CASSIO enter.

IAGO

> There's no other way. She's the one who's got to do it. And what luck, she's here! Go ahead and ask her.

DESDEMONA

> Hello, Cassio. How are you?

CASSIO

> Nothing, madam. Just my earlier request. I'm begging you to help me get back on his good side. I'm devoted to him with all my heart. I can't wait any longer. If my wrongdoing was so serious that I can't get back into his good graces either by my past service, or my present situation, or the promise of devoted service in the future, just knowing that would help me. Then I could stop wondering, and find some other career.

DESDEMONA
                          Alas, thrice-gentle Cassio,
My advocation is not now in tune.
My lord is not my lord, nor should I know him
120   Were he in favor as in humor altered.
So help me every spirit sanctified
As I have spoken for you all my best
And stood within the blank of his displeasure
For my free speech. You must awhile be patient.
125   What I can do I will, and more I will
Than for myself I dare. Let that suffice you.

IAGO
Is my lord angry?

EMILIA
                          He went hence but now,
And certainly in strange unquietness.

IAGO
Can he be angry? I have seen the cannon
130   When it hath blown his ranks into the air
And, like the devil, from his very arm
Puffed his own brother—and is he angry?
Something of moment then, I will go meet him.
There's matter in 't indeed, if he be angry.

DESDEMONA
135   I prithee, do so.

                                        Exit IAGO

                          Something, sure, of state,
Either from Venice, or some unhatched practice
Made demonstrable here in Cyprus to him,
Hath puddled his clear spirit, and in such cases
Men's natures wrangle with inferior things,
140   Though great ones are their object. 'Tis even so,
For let our finger ache and it endues
Our other healthful members even to that sense
Of pain. Nay, we must think men are not gods,

DESDEMONA

I'm sorry, dear Cassio, but now is not the right time to bring up your case. My husband's not himself. If his face changed as much as his personality has, I wouldn't recognize him. God knows I have done my best to argue for you, and made him angry at me for being so aggressive. You'll just have to be patient for a little while. I'll do what I can, more than I'd do for myself. Let that be enough for you.

IAGO

Is Othello angry?

EMILIA

He just left, clearly upset about something.

IAGO

Can he even get angry? It's hard to believe. I've seen him stay calm when cannons were blowing his soldiers to bits, even killing his own brother without him batting an eyelid—is he really upset? It must be about something important. I'll go talk to him. If he's angry, there must be something seriously wrong.

DESDEMONA

Please, do so.

IAGO exits.

There must be some political news from Venice, or some dangerous plot here in Cyprus has ruined his good mood. Men always get angry about little things when they're really worried about bigger ones. That's the way it goes. When our finger hurts, it makes the rest of the body hurt too. We shouldn't expect men to

Nor of them look for such observances
145   As fit the bridal. Beshrew me much, Emilia,
I was, unhandsome warrior as I am,
Arraigning his unkindness with my soul,
But now I find I had suborned the witness,
And he's indicted falsely.

EMILIA

Pray heaven it be
150   State matters, as you think, and no conception
Nor no jealous toy concerning you.

DESDEMONA
Alas the day! I never gave him cause.

EMILIA
But jealous souls will not be answered so.
They are not ever jealous for the cause,
155   But jealous for they're jealous. It is a monster
Begot upon itself, born on itself.

DESDEMONA
Heaven keep the monster from Othello's mind!

EMILIA
Lady, amen.

DESDEMONA
I will go seek him.—Cassio, walk hereabout.
160   If I do find him fit, I'll move your suit
And seek to effect it to my uttermost.

CASSIO
I humbly thank your ladyship.

Exeunt DESDEMONA *and* EMILIA

Enter BIANCA

BIANCA
Save you, friend Cassio!

be perfect, or for them to be as polite as on the wedding day. Oh, Emilia, I'm so inexperienced that I thought he was being unkind, but actually I was judging him harshly.

EMILIA

I hope to God it's something political, like you think, and not jealousy involving you.

DESDEMONA

Oh no! I never gave him reason to be jealous.

EMILIA

But jealous people don't think like that. They're never jealous for a reason; they're just jealous. It's like a monster that just grows and grows, out of nothing.

DESDEMONA

I hope God keeps that monster from growing in Othello's mind!

EMILIA

Amen to that, lady.

DESDEMONA

I'll go look for him—Cassio, stay around here. If he's in a good mood I'll mention you again, and do everything I can.

CASSIO

I thank you, lady.

> DESDEMONA *and* EMILIA *exit.*
BIANCA *enters.*

BIANCA

Hello, Cassio!

CASSIO
What make you from home?
How is 't with you, my most fair Bianca?

165   Indeed, sweet love, I was coming to your house.

BIANCA
And I was going to your lodging, Cassio.
What, keep a week away? Seven days and nights?
Eight score eight hours? And lovers' absent hours
More tedious than the dial eightscore times!

170   Oh weary reckoning!

CASSIO
Pardon me, Bianca,
I have this while with leaden thoughts been pressed,
But I shall, in a more continuate time,
Strike off this score of absence. Sweet Bianca,
(giving her DESDEMONA*'s handkerchief)*
Take me this work out.

BIANCA
O Cassio, whence came this?

175   This is some token from a newer friend!
To the felt absence now I feel a cause.
Is 't come to this? Well, well.

CASSIO
Go to, woman,
Throw your vile guesses in the devil's teeth
From whence you have them. You are jealous now

180   That this is from some mistress, some remembrance.
No, in good troth, Bianca.

BIANCA
Why, whose is it?

CASSIO
I know not neither, I found it in my chamber.
I like the work well. Ere it be demanded,
As like enough it will, I would have it copied.

185   Take it and do 't, and leave me for this time.

BIANCA
Leave you! Wherefore?

CASSIO

Why are you so far from home? How are you, my pretty Bianca? To tell you the truth, I was just going to your house.

BIANCA

And I was just going to yours. You've kept away from me for a week? Seven days and seven nights? A hundred and sixty-eight hours? And lovers' hours are a hundred and sixty times longer than normal ones! What a tedious wait!

CASSIO

I'm sorry, Bianca. All this time I've been depressed and had problems on my mind. When I get some free time I'll make it up to you. *(he gives her* DESDEMONA*'s handkerchief)* Sweet Bianca, would you copy this embroidery pattern for me?

BIANCA

Oh, Cassio, where did you get this? This is a gift from another woman, a new lover! Now I know why you've been staying away from me. Has it come to this? Well, well.

CASSIO

Oh, come on, woman. Stop jumping to silly conclusions. Now you're jealous, thinking that this is from some mistress of mine, but I swear it's not, Bianca.

BIANCA

Well, whose is it?

CASSIO

I don't even know. I found it in my room. It's pretty. Someone is certainly looking for it, and I'll have to give it back. So I'd like it copied. Take it and do that for me, and leave me alone for a while.

BIANCA

Leave you alone! Why?

CASSIO
I do attend here on the general
And think it no addition, nor my wish,
To have him see me womaned.

BIANCA
Why, I pray you?

CASSIO
190   Not that I love you not.

BIANCA
But that you do not love me.
I pray you bring me on the way a little
And say if I shall see you soon at night.

CASSIO
'Tis but a little way that I can bring you,
For I attend here. But I'll see you soon.

BIANCA
195   'Tis very good. I must be circumstanced.

Exeunt

CASSIO

I'm waiting here for the general, and I don't want him to see me with a woman.

BIANCA

And why's that?

CASSIO

It's not because I don't love you.

BIANCA

But you don't love me. Please, just walk with me a little ways, and tell me if I'll see you later tonight.

CASSIO

I can only walk a little way with you, since I'm waiting here. But I'll see you soon.

BIANCA

All right, have it your way. I have to make do.

They exit.

ACT FOUR
SCENE 1

Enter OTHELLO *and* IAGO

IAGO
Will you think so?

OTHELLO
Think so, Iago?

IAGO
What,
To kiss in private?

OTHELLO
An unauthorized kiss!

IAGO
Or to be naked with her friend in bed
An hour or more, not meaning any harm?

OTHELLO
5 Naked in bed, Iago, and not mean harm!
It is hypocrisy against the devil.
They that mean virtuously, and yet do so,
The devil their virtue tempts, and they tempt heaven.

IAGO
So they do nothing, 'tis a venial slip.
10 But if I give my wife a handkerchief—

OTHELLO
What then?

IAGO
Why then 'tis hers, my lord, and, being hers,
She may, I think, bestow 't on any man.

OTHELLO
She is protectress of her honor too.
15 May she give that?

ACT FOUR

SCENE 1

OTHELLO *and* IAGO *enter.*

IAGO

Do you really think so?

OTHELLO

What do you mean, do I think so?

IAGO

What, just because they kissed in private?

OTHELLO

An illicit kiss!

IAGO

Maybe she was just naked in bed with him for an hour or so, but they didn't do anything.

OTHELLO

Naked in bed together, but without doing anything? Come on, Iago. That would be like playing a trick on the devil: they'd make him think they're going to commit adultery, but then back off. Anyone who acted like that would be letting the devil tempt them, and tempting God to condemn them.

IAGO

As long as they didn't do anything, it would only be a minor sin. But if I gave my wife a handkerchief—

OTHELLO

Then what?

IAGO

Then it's hers. And if it's hers, I guess she can give it to any man she wants.

OTHELLO

Her reputation is also her own. Can she give that away too?

IAGO

Her honor is an essence that's not seen,
They have it very oft that have it not.
But for the handkerchief—

OTHELLO

By heaven, I would most gladly have forgot it.
20 Thou saidst—Oh, it comes o'er my memory,
As doth the raven o'er the infectious house,
Boding to all—he had my handkerchief.

IAGO

Ay, what of that?

OTHELLO

                      That's not so good now.

IAGO

What if I had said I had seen him do you wrong?
25 Or heard him say—as knaves be such abroad,
Who having, by their own importunate suit,
Or voluntary dotage of some mistress,
Convincèd or supplied them, cannot choose
But they must blab—

OTHELLO

                      Hath he said any thing?

IAGO

30 He hath, my lord, but be you well assured
No more than he'll unswear.

OTHELLO

                      What hath he said?

IAGO

Why, that he did—I know not what he did.

OTHELLO

What? what?

IAGO

              Lie—

OTHELLO

              With her?

IAGO

You can't see a reputation. A lot of people don't even deserve the reputations they have. But a handkerchief—

OTHELLO

God, I wish I could forget about the handkerchief! What you told me it haunts me like a nightmare—he's got my handkerchief!

IAGO

Yes, what about it?

OTHELLO

That's not good.

IAGO

What if I'd said I saw him do something to hurt you? Or heard him say something about it. You know there are jerks out there who have to brag about bedding some woman.—

OTHELLO

Has he said anything?

IAGO

Yes, but he'd deny it all.

OTHELLO

What did he say?

IAGO

He said he did—I don't know.

OTHELLO

He what?

IAGO

He was in bed with—

OTHELLO

With her?

IAGO

With her, on her, what you will.

OTHELLO

Lie with her? lie on her? We say "lie on her" when they
35 belie her! Lie with her—that's fulsome. Handkerchief—
confessions—handkerchief! To confess, and be hanged
for his labor. First to be hanged, and then to confess—I
tremble at it. Nature would not invest herself in such
shadowing passion without some instruction. It is not
40 words that shake me thus. Pish! Noses, ears, and lips. Is 't
possible? Confess!—Handkerchief!—Oh, devil!—
(falls in a trance)

IAGO

Work on, My medicine, work! Thus credulous fools are
caught,
And many worthy and chaste dames even thus,
All guiltless, meet reproach.—What, ho! My lord!
45 My lord, I say! Othello!

Enter **CASSIO**

How now, Cassio!

CASSIO

What's the matter?

IAGO

My lord is fall'n into an epilepsy.
This is his second fit. He had one yesterday.

CASSIO

Rub him about the temples.

IAGO

No, forbear.
50 The lethargy must have his quiet course.
If not, he foams at mouth and by and by
Breaks out to savage madness. Look, he stirs.
Do you withdraw yourself a little while,

IAGO

With her, on top of her—however you want to say it.

OTHELLO

In bed with her? On top of her? I would have thought people were telling lies about her rather than believe he was lying on her. My God, it's nauseating! Handkerchief—confessions—handkerchief! I'll kill him first, and then let him confess—I'm trembling with rage. I wouldn't be trembling like this if I didn't know deep down this was all true. Noses, ears, lips. Is it possible? Tell me the truth—Handkerchief—Damn it!
(he falls into a trance)

IAGO

Keep working, poison! This is the way to trick gullible fools. Many good and innocent women are punished for reasons like this.—My lord? My lord, Othello!

CASSIO *enters.*

Hey, Cassio!

CASSIO

What's the matter?

IAGO

Othello's having some kind of epileptic fit. This is his second fit like this. He had one yesterday.

CASSIO

Rub his temples.

IAGO

No, don't. This fit has to run its course. If you interrupt it, he'll foam at the mouth and go crazy. Look, he's moving. Why don't you go away for a bit? He'll

He will recover straight. When he is gone
55   I would on great occasion speak with you.

Exit CASSIO

How is it, general? Have you not hurt your head?

OTHELLO
Dost thou mock me?

IAGO
                 I mock you not, by heaven.
Would you would bear your fortune like a man!

OTHELLO
A hornèd man's a monster and a beast.

IAGO
60   There's many a beast then in a populous city,
And many a civil monster.

OTHELLO
Did he confess it?

IAGO
              Good sir, be a man,
Think every bearded fellow that's but yoked
May draw with you. There's millions now alive
65   That nightly lie in those unproper beds
Which they dare swear peculiar. Your case is better.
Oh, 'tis the spite of hell, the fiend's arch-mock,
To lip a wanton in a secure couch,
And to suppose her chaste. No, let me know,
70   And knowing what I am, I know what she shall be.

OTHELLO
Oh, thou art wise! 'Tis certain.

IAGO
                   Stand you awhile apart,
Confine yourself but in a patient list.
Whilst you were here o'erwhelmèd with your grief—
A passion most resulting such a man—
75   Cassio came hither. I shifted him away
And laid good 'scuses upon your ecstasy,

get better right away. When he leaves, it's very important that I talk to you.

CASSIO *exits.*

What happened, general? Did you hit your head?

OTHELLO

Are you making fun of me?

IAGO

Making fun of you? No, I swear! I wish you could face your bad news like a man!

OTHELLO

A man who's been cheated on isn't a real man. He's subhuman, like an animal.

IAGO

In that case there are a lot of animals on the loose in this city.

OTHELLO

Did he confess?

IAGO

Sir, be a man. Every married man has been cheated on. Millions of men sleep with wives who cheat on them, wrongly believing they belong to them alone. Your case is better than that. At least you're not ignorant. The worst thing of all is to kiss your wife thinking she's innocent, when in fact she's a whore. No, I'd rather know the truth. Then I'll know exactly what she is, just as I know what I am.

OTHELLO

You're wise! That's for sure.

IAGO

Go somewhere else for a while. Calm down. While you were dazed by grief—which isn't appropriate for a man like you—Cassio showed up here. I got him to leave, and made up an excuse for your trance. I told him to come back and talk to me in a bit, and he promised he would. So hide here and watch how he sneers

Bade him anon return and here speak with me,
The which he promised. Do but encave yourself,
And mark the fleers, the gibes, and notable scorns
80   That dwell in every region of his face.
For I will make him tell the tale anew
Where, how, how oft, how long ago, and when
He hath, and is again to cope your wife.
I say, but mark his gesture. Marry, patience,
85   Or I shall say you are all in all in spleen,
And nothing of a man.

OTHELLO

                                    Dost thou hear, Iago?
I will be found most cunning in my patience,
But—dost thou hear?—most bloody.

IAGO

                                         That's not amiss,
But yet keep time in all. Will you withdraw?

OTHELLO *withdraws*

90   Now will I question Cassio of Bianca,
A huswife that by selling her desires
Buys herself bread and clothes. It is a creature
That dotes on Cassio, as 'tis the strumpet's plague
To beguile many and be beguiled by one.
95   He, when he hears of her, cannot refrain
From the excess of laughter. Here he comes.

Enter **CASSIO**

As he shall smile, Othello shall go mad.
And his unbookish jealousy must construe
Poor Cassio's smiles, gestures, and light behavior
100   Quite in the wrong.—How do you now, lieutenant?

at you. I'll make him tell me the whole story again—
where, how often, how long ago—and when he plans
to sleep with your wife in the future. I'm telling you,
just watch his face. But stay calm, and don't get carried away by rage, or I'll think you're not a man.

OTHELLO

Do you hear what I'm saying, Iago? I'll be very patient,
but—do you hear me?—I'm not done with him yet

IAGO

That's fine, but for now keep your cool. Will you go
hide?

OTHELLO *hides.*

Now I'll ask Cassio about Bianca, a prostitute who
sells her body for food and clothes. She's crazy about
Cassio. That's the whore's curse, to seduce many men,
but to be seduced by one. Whenever he talks about her
he can't stop laughing.

CASSIO *enters.*

And when he laughs, Othello will go crazy. In his
ignorant jealousy, he'll totally misunderstand Cassio's smiles, gestures, and jokes.—How are you, lieutenant?

CASSIO

> The worser that you give me the addition
> Whose want even kills me.

IAGO

> Ply Desdemona well, and you are sure on 't.
> Now if this suit lay in Bianca's power
> 105   How quickly should you speed!

CASSIO

>   Alas, poor caitiff!

OTHELLO

> Look how he laughs already!

IAGO

> I never knew woman love man so.

CASSIO

> Alas, poor rogue, I think indeed she loves me.

OTHELLO

> Now he denies it faintly, and laughs it out.

IAGO

> 110   Do you hear, Cassio?

OTHELLO

>   Now he importunes him
> To tell it o'er. Go to, well said, well said.

IAGO

> She gives it out that you shall marry her.
> Do you intend it?

CASSIO

> Ha, ha, ha!

OTHELLO

> 115   Do ye triumph, Roman? Do you triumph?

CASSIO

> I marry her! What? A customer? Prithee bear some
> charity to my wit. Do not think it so unwholesome. Ha,
> ha, ha!

OTHELLO

> So, so, so, so! They laugh that win!

CASSIO

It doesn't make me feel any better when you call me lieutenant. I'm dying to have that title back again.

IAGO

Just keep asking Desdemona, and it'll be yours. If it was up to Bianca to get you your job back, you'd have had it already!

CASSIO

The poor thing!

OTHELLO

He's laughing already!

IAGO

I never knew a woman who loved a man so much.

CASSIO

The poor thing, I really think she loves me.

OTHELLO

Now he denies it a bit, and tries to laugh it off.

IAGO

Have you heard this, Cassio?

OTHELLO

He's asking him to tell the story again. Go on, tell it.

IAGO

She says you're going to marry her. Are you?

CASSIO

Ha, ha, ha!

OTHELLO

Are you laughing because you've won? Do you think you've won?

CASSIO

Me, marry her? That whore? Please give me a little credit! I'm not that stupid. Ha, ha, ha!

OTHELLO

So, so, so, so! The winner's always got the last laugh, hasn't he?

IAGO

120   Why the cry goes that you shall marry her.

CASSIO

Prithee say true!

IAGO

I am a very villain else.

OTHELLO

Have you scored me? Well.

CASSIO

This is the monkey's own giving out. She is persuaded I
125   will marry her, out of her own love and flattery, not out of
my promise.

OTHELLO

Iago beckons me. Now he begins the story.

CASSIO

She was here even now. She haunts me in every place. I
was the other day talking on the sea-bank with certain
130   Venetians, and thither comes the bauble and, by this
hand, she falls me thus about my neck—

OTHELLO

Crying "O dear Cassio!" as it were. His gesture imports it.

CASSIO

So hangs and lolls and weeps upon me, so shakes, and
pulls me! Ha, ha, ha!

OTHELLO

135   Now he tells how she plucked him to my chamber. Oh, I
see that nose of yours, but not that dog I shall throw it to.

CASSIO

Well, I must leave her company.

IAGO

Before me! Look, where she comes.

Enter BIANCA

IAGO

I swear, there's a rumor going around that you'll marry her.

CASSIO

You're kidding!

IAGO

If it's not true, you can call me a villain.

OTHELLO

Have you given me bastard children to raise? All right, then.

CASSIO

The little monkey must have started that rumor herself. She thinks I'll marry her because she loves me. She's just flattering herself. I never promised her anything.

OTHELLO

Iago is gesturing for me to come closer. Now he's telling the story.

CASSIO

She was here just now. She hangs around me all the time. I was talking to some Venetians down by the shore, and the fool showed up. I swear to you, she put her arms around me like this—

OTHELLO

Saying, "Oh, Cassio," it seems, judging by his gestures.

CASSIO

She hangs around me and dangles from my neck and cries, shaking me and pulling at me. Ha, ha, ha!

OTHELLO

Now he's saying how she took him into our bedroom. Oh, I can see your nose now. But I can't see the dog I'm going to throw it to.

CASSIO

I have to get rid of her.

IAGO

Look out, here she comes.

BIANCA *enters.*

CASSIO

'Tis such another fitchew. Marry, a perfumed one.—
140   What do you mean by this haunting of me?

BIANCA

Let the devil and his dam haunt you! What did you
mean by that same handkerchief you gave me even now?
I was a fine fool to take it. I must take out the
work? A likely piece of work, that you should find
145   it in your chamber, and not know who left it there!
This is some minx's token, and I must take out the
work? There, give it your hobby-horse. Wheresoever
you had it, I'll take out no work on 't.

CASSIO

How now, my sweet Bianca! How now, how now?

OTHELLO

150   By heaven, that should be my handkerchief!

BIANCA

If you'll come to supper tonight, you may. If you will not,
come when you are next prepared for.

Exit

IAGO

After her, after her.

CASSIO

I must, she'll rail in the street else.

IAGO

155   Will you sup there?

CASSIO

Yes, I intend so.

IAGO

Well, I may chance to see you, for I would very fain
speak with you.

CASSIO

Prithee come, will you?

IAGO

160   Go to! Say no more.

Exit CASSIO

CASSIO

It's a whore like all the others, stinking of cheap perfume.—Why are you always hanging around me?

BIANCA

Damn you! What did you mean by giving me this handkerchief? I was an idiot to take it! You want me to copy the embroidery pattern? That was a likely story, that you found it in your room and didn't know who it belonged to. This is a love token from some other slut, and you want me to copy its pattern for you? Give it back to her, I won't do anything with it.

CASSIO

What is it, my dear Bianca? What's wrong?

OTHELLO

My God, that's my handkerchief!

BIANCA

If you want to come have dinner with me, you can. If you don't want to, then good riddance.

BIANCA exits.

IAGO

Go after her, go.

CASSIO

Actually, I should. She'll scream in the streets if I don't.

IAGO

Will you be having dinner with her tonight?

CASSIO

Yes, I will.

IAGO

Well, maybe I'll see you there. I'd really like to speak with you.

CASSIO

Please come. Will you?

IAGO

Don't talk anymore, go after her.

CASSIO exits.

OTHELLO

    (advancing) How shall I murder him, Iago?

IAGO

    Did you perceive how he laughed at his vice?

OTHELLO

    O Iago!

IAGO

    And did you see the handkerchief?

OTHELLO

165   Was that mine?

IAGO

    Yours by this hand. And to see how he prizes the foolish woman your wife! She gave it him, and he hath given it his whore.

OTHELLO

    I would have him nine years a-killing. A fine woman! A
170   fair woman! A sweet woman!

IAGO

    Nay, you must forget that.

OTHELLO

    Ay, let her rot and perish and be damned tonight, for she shall not live. No, my heart is turned to stone. I strike it and it hurts my hand. Oh, the world hath not a sweeter
175   creature, she might lie by an emperor's side and command him tasks.

IAGO

    Nay, that's not your way.

OTHELLO

    Hang her! I do but say what she is. So delicate with her needle, an admirable musician. Oh, she will sing the
180   savageness out of a bear! Of so high and plenteous wit and invention!

IAGO

    She's the worse for all this.

OTHELLO

(coming forward) How should I murder him, Iago?

IAGO

Did you see how he laughed about sleeping with her?

OTHELLO

Oh Iago!

IAGO

And did you see the handkerchief?

OTHELLO

Was it mine?

IAGO

It was yours, I swear. And do you see how much your foolish wife means to him? She gave it to him, and he gave it to his whore.

OTHELLO

I wish I could keep killing him for nine years straight. Oh, she's a fine woman! A fair woman! A sweet woman!

IAGO

No, you have to forget all that now.

OTHELLO

Yes, let her die and rot and go to hell tonight. She won't stay alive for long. No, my heart's turned to stone—when I hit it, it hurts my hand. Oh, the world never saw a sweeter creature. She could be married to an emperor, and he'd be like her slave!

IAGO

But that's not how you're going to be.

OTHELLO

Damn her, I'm just describing her truthfully! She's so good at sewing, and a wonderful musician. Oh, she could sing a wild bear to sleep! Oh, she's so witty and creative!

IAGO

All the worse that she stooped this low, then.

OTHELLO

Oh, a thousand thousand times—and then of so gentle a condition!

IAGO

185   Ay, too gentle.

OTHELLO

Nay, that's certain. But yet the pity of it, Iago! O Iago, the pity of it, Iago!

IAGO

If you are so fond over her iniquity, give her patent to offend, for if it touch not you it comes near nobody.

OTHELLO

190   I will chop her into messes! Cuckold me?

IAGO

Oh, 'tis foul in her.

OTHELLO

With mine officer!

IAGO

That's fouler.

OTHELLO

Get me some poison, Iago, this night. I'll not expostulate
195   with her, lest her body and beauty unprovide my mind again—This night, Iago!

IAGO

Do it not with poison. Strangle her in her bed, even the bed she hath contaminated.

OTHELLO

Good, good, the justice of it pleases! Very good!

IAGO

200   And for Cassio, let me be his undertaker. You shall hear more by midnight.

OTHELLO

Excellent good.

A trumpet within

OTHELLO

Oh, a thousand times worse, a thousand times—and what a sweet personality she has!

IAGO

Yes, a little too sweet.

OTHELLO

Yes, that's for sure. Oh, it's dreadful, dreadful, Iago!

IAGO

If you still feel so affectionate toward her, then why not give her permission to cheat on you? If it doesn't bother you, it won't bother anyone else.

OTHELLO

I'll chop her into pieces. How could she cheat on me?

IAGO

Oh, it's horrible of her.

OTHELLO

And with my own officer!

IAGO

That's worse.

OTHELLO

Get me some poison tonight, Iago. I won't argue with her, so her beautiful body won't disarm me.— Tonight, Iago.

IAGO

Don't do it with poison. Strangle her in her bed, the same bed she's contaminated.

OTHELLO

Good, good, I like that—it's only fair! Very good!

IAGO

And let me kill Cassio. You'll hear more from me by midnight.

OTHELLO

Excellent, good.

A trumpet sounds offstage.

What trumpet is that same?

IAGO

I warrant something from Venice. 'Tis Lodovico, this,
205   comes from the duke. See, your wife's with him.

Enter LODOVICO, DESDEMONA, *and attendants*

LODOVICO

Save you, worthy general!

OTHELLO

With all my heart, sir.

LODOVICO

The duke and senators of Venice greet you.
(gives him a letter)

OTHELLO

I kiss the instrument of their pleasures.

DESDEMONA

210   And what's the news, good cousin Lodovico?

IAGO

I am very glad to see you, signior. Welcome to Cyprus.

LODOVICO

I thank you. How does lieutenant Cassio?

IAGO

Lives, sir.

DESDEMONA

Cousin, there's fall'n between him and my lord
215   An unkind breach, but you shall make all well.

OTHELLO

Are you sure of that?

DESDEMONA

My lord?

OTHELLO

(reads) "This fail you not to do, as you will—"

What's that trumpet for?

IAGO

I think someone's coming from Venice. It's Lodovico. He must be coming from the duke. Look, your wife is with him.

LODOVICO, DESDEMONA *and attendants enter.*

LODOVICO

Greetings, good general!

OTHELLO

Greetings, sir.

LODOVICO

The duke and senators of Venice greet you.
(he hands OTHELLO *a piece of paper)*

OTHELLO

I'll do whatever they order me to do in this letter.

DESDEMONA

What's new, cousin Lodovico?

IAGO

Very nice to see you, sir. Welcome to Cyprus.

LODOVICO

Thank you. How is lieutenant Cassio?

IAGO

Well, he's alive.

DESDEMONA

Cousin, there's been a falling out between him and Othello. An unfortunate rift, but you can fix it.

OTHELLO

Are you sure of that?

DESDEMONA

Excuse me?

OTHELLO

(reading) "Don't fail to do this, since you'll—"

LODOVICO
He did not call, he's busy in the paper.
220   Is there division 'twixt my lord and Cassio?

DESDEMONA
A most unhappy one. I would do much
T' atone them, for the love I bear to Cassio.

OTHELLO
Fire and brimstone!

DESDEMONA
My lord?

OTHELLO
Are you wise?

DESDEMONA
What, is he angry?

LODOVICO
Maybe the letter moved him,
225   For, as I think, they do command him home,
Deputing Cassio in his government.

DESDEMONA
Trust me, I am glad on 't.

OTHELLO
Indeed!

DESDEMONA
My lord?

OTHELLO
230   I am glad to see you mad.

DESDEMONA
Why, sweet Othello—

OTHELLO
(striking her) Devil!

DESDEMONA
I have not deserved this.

LODOVICO

He didn't say anything, he's reading. So there's a rift between Othello and Cassio?

DESDEMONA

Yes, unfortunately. I'd do anything to bring them back together, since I really care for Cassio.

OTHELLO

Damn it all!

DESDEMONA

Excuse me, my lord?

OTHELLO

Are you in your right mind?

DESDEMONA

Is he angry?

LODOVICO

Maybe the letter upset him. I think they want him to go home and appoint Cassio governor in his place.

DESDEMONA

I'm happy about that.

OTHELLO

Oh, are you really!

DESDEMONA

My lord?

OTHELLO

I'm glad you're insane enough to admit it in front of me.

DESDEMONA

Why, sweet Othello—

OTHELLO

(striking her) You devil!

DESDEMONA

I haven't done anything to deserve this!

LODOVICO

    My lord, this would not be believed in Venice,

235   Though I should swear I saw 't. 'Tis very much.

    Make her amends, she weeps.

OTHELLO

                      Oh, devil, devil!

    If that the earth could teem with woman's tears,

    Each drop she falls would prove a crocodile.

    Out of my sight!

DESDEMONA

240   I will not stay to offend you.

LODOVICO

    Truly, an obedient lady.

    I do beseech your lordship, call her back.

OTHELLO

    Mistress!

DESDEMONA

    My lord?

OTHELLO

245   What would you with her, sir?

LODOVICO

    Who, I, my lord?

OTHELLO

    Ay, you did wish that I would make her turn.

    Sir, she can turn, and turn, and yet go on,

    And turn again. And she can weep, sir, weep.

250   And she's obedient, as you say, obedient,

    Very obedient.—Proceed you in your tears.—

    Concerning this, sir—Oh, well-painted passion!—

    I am commanded home.—Get you away,

    I'll send for you anon.—Sir, I obey the mandate

255   And will return to Venice.—Hence, avaunt!

Exit DESDEMONA

LODOVICO

My lord, no one will believe this in Venice, even though I'd swear I saw it with my own eyes. That was too much. You should apologize. She's crying.

OTHELLO

Oh, you devil, you devil! You can cry all day and all night, and I still won't believe you're sad. Get out of my sight!

DESDEMONA

I wouldn't want to stay here and make you angry.

LODOVICO

She's obedient—a fine lady. Please, my lord, call her back.

OTHELLO

Madam!

DESDEMONA

My lord?

OTHELLO

What do you want with her, sir?

LODOVICO

Who, me?

OTHELLO

Yes, you asked me to call her back. See how well she can turn? She can turn and turn, and then turn on you again. And she can cry, sir—oh, how she can cry! And she's obedient, as you say, obedient. Very obedient— keep crying.—Concerning this—oh, what fake emotion!—I am being ordered home—Get away from me, I'll send for you later.—Sir, I'll obey the order and return to Venice. Get away from me, you witch!

DESDEMONA exits.

Cassio shall have my place. And, sir, tonight
I do entreat that we may sup together.
You are welcome, sir, to Cyprus. Goats and monkeys!

Exit

LODOVICO

Is this the noble Moor whom our full senate
260 Call all in all sufficient? Is this the nature
Whom passion could not shake? Whose solid virtue
The shot of accident nor dart of chance
Could neither graze nor pierce?

IAGO

He is much changed.

LODOVICO

Are his wits safe? Is he not light of brain?

IAGO

265 He's that he is. I may not breathe my censure
What he might be. If what he might he is not,
I would to heaven he were!

LODOVICO

What? Strike his wife?

IAGO

'Faith, that was not so well. Yet would I knew
That stroke would prove the worst!

LODOVICO

Is it his use?
270 Or did the letters work upon his blood
And new-create his fault?

Cassio can have my job. And tonight, sir, I invite you have dinner with me. Welcome to Cyprus. Horny animals!

OTHELLO *exits.*

LODOVICO

Is this the same Moor whom the senate considers so capable? Is this the guy who's supposed to never get emotional, and who never gets rattled, no matter what disaster happens?

IAGO

He's changed a great deal.

LODVICO

Is he sane? Is he losing his mind?

IAGO

He is what he is. I won't say anything negative about what he might be. If he isn't what he might be, then I wish to God he were!

LODOVICO

Hitting his wife?

IAGO

It's true, that wasn't such a nice thing to do. But I wish I could say that's the last time he'll do it!

LODOVICO

Is it a habit of his? Or did the letter make him emotional somehow, and this is the first time he's done it?

IAGO
                                        Alas, alas!
It is not honesty in me to speak
What I have seen and known. You shall observe him,
And his own courses will denote him so
275   That I may save my speech. Do but go after
And mark how he continues.

LODOVICO
I am sorry that I am deceived in him.

                                                        Exeunt

IAGO

Oh, it's too bad! It wouldn't be right for me to tell you everything I've seen and heard. You'll see what he's like. His own actions will show you what kind of person he is, so I won't have to bother telling you. Just go after him and watch what he does next.

LODOVICO

I'm sorry I was so wrong about him.

They exit.

ACT 4, SCENE 2

Enter OTHELLO *and* EMILIA

OTHELLO
You have seen nothing then?

EMILIA
Nor ever heard, nor ever did suspect.

OTHELLO
Yes, you have seen Cassio and she together.

EMILIA
But then I saw no harm, and then I heard
5   Each syllable that breath made up between them.

OTHELLO
What, did they never whisper?

EMILIA
Never, my lord.

OTHELLO
Nor send you out o' th' way?

EMILIA
Never.

OTHELLO
10   To fetch her fan, her gloves, her mask, nor nothing?

EMILIA
Never, my lord.

OTHELLO
That's strange.

EMILIA
I durst, my lord, to wager she is honest,
Lay down my soul at stake. If you think other
15   Remove your thought, it doth abuse your bosom.
If any wretch have put this in your head
Let heaven requite it with the serpent's curse
For if she be not honest, chaste, and true
There's no man happy. The purest of their wives
20   Is foul as slander.

ACT 4, SCENE 2

OTHELLO *and* EMILIA *enter.*

OTHELLO

You haven't seen anything, then?

EMILIA

No, and I didn't hear anything either, or suspect anything at all.

OTHELLO

But you've seen her and Cassio together.

EMILIA

Yes, but I didn't see anything wrong, and I heard every syllable they said.

OTHELLO

Didn't they ever whisper?

EMILIA

Never, my lord.

OTHELLO

Or ask you to leave the room?

EMILIA

Never.

OTHELLO

Not even to get her fan, or her gloves, or her mask, or anything?

EMILIA

No, my lord.

OTHELLO

That's strange.

EMILIA

I'd swear to you on my soul that she's a good, honest person, sir. If you suspect otherwise, stop thinking that right now because you're wrong. If any jerk has tried to convince you she's bad, I hope God curses him. If she's not honest, faithful, and true, then there's no such thing as a faithful wife or a happy husband.

OTHELLO

Bid her come hither. Go.

Exit EMILIA

She says enough, yet she's a simple bawd
That cannot say as much. This is a subtle whore,
A closet, lock and key, of villainous secrets.
25   And yet she'll kneel and pray, I have seen her do 't.

Enter DESDEMONA *with* EMILIA

DESDEMONA
My lord, what is your will?

OTHELLO
Pray, chuck, come hither.

DESDEMONA
What is your pleasure?

OTHELLO

Let me see your eyes.

Look in my face.

DESDEMONA

What horrible fancy's this?

OTHELLO
30   (*to* EMILIA) Some of your function, mistress,
Leave procreants alone and shut the door.
Cough or cry "hem" if any body come.
Your mystery, your mystery! Nay, dispatch!

. *Exit* EMILIA

DESDEMONA
Upon my knee, what doth your speech import?
35   I understand a fury in your words,
But not the words.

OTHELLO

Why, what art thou?

OTHELLO

Tell her to come here. Go.

EMILIA exits.

She says all the right things, but the dumbest brothel-keeper would tell the same story. Desdemona's a tricky whore with a closet full of awful secrets, but still she'll kneel and pray like an honest woman. I've seen her do it.

DESDEMONA and EMILIA enter.

DESDEMONA

My lord, what do you want?

OTHELLO

Please, dear, come here.

DESDEMONA

What can I do for you?

OTHELLO

Let me see your eyes. Look at my face.

DESDEMONA

What horrible thing are you imagining?

OTHELLO

(to EMILIA) Go do what you do best, madam. Leave us alone for our hanky-panky, and shut the door behind you. If somebody comes, give a shout. That's your job, your job. Go on, hurry!

EMILIA exits.

Othello implies that Emilia's job is to help men and women have illicit sex.

DESDEMONA

I'm begging you on my knees to tell me what your words mean. I can tell you're furious, but I don't understand what you're saying.

OTHELLO

Why? Who are you?

DESDEMONA

Your wife, my lord. Your true and loyal wife.

OTHELLO

Come, swear it, damn thyself.

Lest, being like one of heaven, the devils themselves

40 Should fear to seize thee. Therefore be double damned,

Swear thou art honest!

DESDEMONA

Heaven doth truly know it.

OTHELLO

Heaven truly knows that thou art false as hell.

DESDEMONA

To whom, my lord? With whom? How am I false?

OTHELLO

Ah, Desdemona, away, away, away!

DESDEMONA

45 Alas the heavy day, why do you weep?

Am I the motive of these tears, my lord?

If haply you my father do suspect

An instrument of this your calling back,

Lay not your blame on me. If you have lost him,

50 Why, I have lost him too.

OTHELLO

Had it pleased heaven

To try me with affliction, had they rained

All kinds of sores and shames on my bare head,

Steeped me in poverty to the very lips,

Given to captivity me and my utmost hopes,

55 I should have found in some place of my soul

A drop of patience. But, alas, to make me

DESDEMONA

I'm your wife, your true and loyal wife.

OTHELLO

Go ahead, swear to that, so you'll be damned to hell for lying. Otherwise the devils will mistake you for an angel and be too scared to grab you. Go ahead, make sure you damn yourself by swearing you've been faithful to me.

DESDEMONA

Heaven knows I am.

OTHELLO

Heaven knows you're as unfaithful as hell.

DESDEMONA

Unfaithful, my lord? With whom? How am I unfaithful?

OTHELLO

Leave me alone, Desdemona, go away!

DESDEMONA

Oh, what a horrible day! Why are you crying? Because of me? If you've been ordered back to Venice because of my father, don't blame me. You may have lost his respect, but so have I.

OTHELLO

If God had decided to treat me like Job, making me sick and covered with sores, reducing me to abject poverty, selling me into slavery and destroying all my hopes, I would have found some way to accept it with patience. But instead He's made me a laughingstock for everyone in our time to point at and scorn! Even that I could put up with. But instead, my wife, who's

The fixèd figure for the time of scorn
To point his slow and moving finger at!
Yet could I bear that too, well, very well.
60 But there where I have garnered up my heart,
Where either I must live or bear no life,
The fountain from the which my current runs
Or else dries up—to be discarded thence!
Or keep it as a cistern for foul toads
65 To knot and gender in! Turn thy complexion there,
Patience, thou young and rose-lipped cherubin,—
Ay, there, look grim as hell!

DESDEMONA
I hope my noble lord esteems me honest.

OTHELLO
Oh, ay, as summer flies are in the shambles,
70 That quicken even with blowing. O thou weed,
Who art so lovely fair and smell'st so sweet
That the sense aches at thee, would thou hadst ne'er been
born!

DESDEMONA
Alas, what ignorant sin have I committed?

OTHELLO
75 Was this fair paper, this most goodly book,
Made to write "whore" upon? What committed?
Committed? O thou public commoner!
I should make very forges of my cheeks
That would to cinders burn up modesty
80 Did I but speak thy deeds. What committed?
Heaven stops the nose at it and the moon winks,
The bawdy wind that kisses all it meets
Is hushed within the hollow mine of earth
And will not hear 't. What committed!
85 Impudent strumpet!

DESDEMONA
By heaven, you do me wrong!

supposed to be like the fountain that my children and all my descendants flow from, has rejected me! Worse than that, she's polluted herself, so that the fountain is a place where disgusting toads copulate and reproduce! Even the goddess of patience couldn't look at this and be patient—it's too horrifying!

DESDEMONA

I hope you think I'm faithful to you.

OTHELLO

As faithful as flies in rotting meat, which give birth to maggots every time the wind blows. You're like a weed pretending to be a flower, so beautiful and sweet-smelling that I ache when I look at you. Oh, I wish you'd never been born!

DESDEMONA

Have I done something to offend you without knowing it?

OTHELLO

Was someone as beautiful as you meant to be a whore? What have you done? What have you done? Oh, you streetwalker! If I said out loud what you've done, you'd burn up with shame. What have you done? Heaven has to hold its nose when it sees you! The pure moon in the sky has to shut its eyes when you go by! Even the wind that blows over everything on earth is ashamed to visit you. You brazen whore!

DESDEMONA

I swear to God you're accusing me wrongly!

OTHELLO
Are you not a strumpet?

DESDEMONA
No, as I am a Christian.
If to preserve this vessel for my lord
90 From any other foul unlawful touch
Be not to be a strumpet, I am none.

OTHELLO
What, not a whore?

DESDEMONA
No, as I shall be saved.

OTHELLO
Is 't possible?

DESDEMONA
Oh, heaven forgive us!

OTHELLO
95 I cry you mercy, then,
I took you for that cunning whore of Venice
That married with Othello.—You, mistress,
That have the office opposite to Saint Peter
And keep the gate of hell!

Enter EMILIA

You, you, ay, you!
100 We have done our course. There's money for your pains.
I pray you, turn the key and keep our counsel.

Exit

EMILIA
Alas, what does this gentleman conceive?
How do you, madam? How do you, my good lady?

DESDEMONA
Faith, half asleep.

EMILIA
105 Good madam, what's the matter with my lord?

OTHELLO

So you're saying you're not a whore?

DESDEMONA

No, I'm as honest as I am Christian. If only letting my husband touch my body means I'm not a whore, I'm not a whore.

OTHELLO

What, you're not a whore?

DESDEMONA

No, I swear it.

OTHELLO

Is that possible?

DESDEMONA

Oh, heaven help us!

OTHELLO

I beg your pardon then. I must have the wrong woman. I mistook you for that sly Venetian woman who married Othello.—You whorehouse-keeper.

EMILIA enters.

You're in charge of this hell! You! We've finished our business. Here's some money for you. Please lock the door and keep quiet.

OTHELLO exits.

EMILIA

What's he talking about? How are you, madam?

DESDEMONA

I'm stunned, to tell you the truth.

EMILIA

My lady, what's wrong with your husband?

DESDEMONA
> With who?

EMILIA
> > Why, with my lord, madam.

DESDEMONA
> Who is thy lord?

EMILIA
> > He that is yours, sweet lady.

DESDEMONA
> I have none. Do not talk to me, Emilia.
> I cannot weep, nor answers have I none,
110 But what should go by water. Prithee, tonight
> Lay on my bed my wedding sheets. Remember,
> And call thy husband hither.

EMILIA
> > Here's a change indeed!

> > *Exit*

DESDEMONA
> 'Tis meet I should be used so, very meet.
> How have I been behaved that he might stick
115 The small'st opinion on my least misuse?

Enter EMILIA *with* IAGO

IAGO
> What is your pleasure, madam? How is 't with you?

DESDEMONA
> I cannot tell. Those that do teach young babes
> Do it with gentle means and easy tasks.
> He might have chid me so, for, in good faith,
120 I am a child to chiding.

IAGO
> > What is the matter, lady?

DESDEMONA

With who?

EMILIA

Why, with your husband, madam. My lord.

DESDEMONA

Who's your lord?

EMILIA

My lord is your lord.

DESDEMONA

I don't have a lord. Don't talk to me, Emilia. I can't even cry, though tears are the only answers I could give to all your questions. Tonight put my wedding sheets on my bed, and tell your husband to come to me now.

EMILIA

Things have certainly changed!

EMILIA exits.

DESDEMONA

It's fair for him to treat me like this, very fair. What have I ever done that he has anything to complain about?

IAGO and EMILIA enter.

IAGO

What can I do for you, madam? How are you?

DESDEMONA

I don't know. When grown-ups teach little children, they do it gently and easily. He might have treated me like that, because I'm as unused to abuse as a little child.

IAGO

What's the matter, lady?

EMILIA
> Alas, Iago, my lord hath so bewhored her,
> Thrown such despite and heavy terms upon her,
> That true hearts cannot bear it.

DESDEMONA
> Am I that name, Iago?

IAGO
125
> What name, fair lady?

DESDEMONA
> Such as she says my lord did say I was.

EMILIA
> He called her "whore." A beggar in his drink
> Could not have laid such terms upon his callet.

IAGO
> Why did he so?

DESDEMONA
130
> I do not know. I am sure I am none such.

IAGO
> Do not weep, do not weep. Alas the day!

EMILIA
> Hath she forsook so many noble matches,
> Her father and her country, and her friends,
> To be called "whore"? Would it not make one weep?

DESDEMONA
135
> It is my wretched fortune.

IAGO
> Beshrew him for 't!
> How comes this trick upon him?

DESDEMONA
> Nay, heaven doth know.

EMILIA
> I will be hanged, if some eternal villain,
> Some busy and insinuating rogue,
> Some cogging, cozening slave, to get some office,
140
> Have not devised this slander. I will be hanged else!

EMILIA

He called her a whore so many times, and heaped up so much abuse on her that good people can't stand to hear it.

DESDEMONA

Am I that name, Iago?

IAGO

What name, madam?

DESDEMONA

What my lord said I was.

EMILIA

He called her a whore. A beggar couldn't have called his slut worse names.

IAGO

Why did he do that?

DESDEMONA

I don't know. I just know I'm not one.

IAGO

Don't cry, don't cry. What a day this is!

EMILIA

Did she give up all those chances to marry noblemen, give up her father and country and friends, just to be called a whore? Doesn't that make you want to cry?

DESDEMONA

It's just my bad luck.

IAGO

Damn him! How did he get such an idea?

DESDEMONA

Heaven knows.

EMILIA

I bet my life some evil busybody, some meddling, lying jerk made up this rumor to get some position. I bet my life on it.

IAGO

Fie, there is no such man. It is impossible.

DESDEMONA

If any such there be, heaven pardon him!

EMILIA

A halter pardon him and hell gnaw his bones!
Why should he call her "whore"? Who keeps her company?
145   What place? What time? What form? What likelihood?
The Moor's abused by some most villainous knave,
Some base notorious knave, some scurvy fellow.
O heavens, that such companions thou'dst unfold,
And put in every honest hand a whip
150   To lash the rascals naked through the world
Even from the east to th' west!

IAGO

                        Speak within door.

EMILIA

Oh, fie upon them! Some such squire he was
That turned your wit the seamy side without
And made you to suspect me with the Moor.

IAGO

155   You are a fool. Go to.

DESDEMONA

                  Alas Iago,
What shall I do to win my lord again?
Good friend, go to him. For, by this light of heaven,
I know not how I lost him. Here I kneel:
If e'er my will did trespass 'gainst his love,
160   Either in discourse of thought or actual deed,
Or that mine eyes, mine ears, or any sense,
Delighted them, or any other form,
Or that I do not yet, and ever did,

IAGO

Nobody's that bad. It's impossible.

DESDEMONA

If there is, then heaven help him!

EMILIA

A hangman's noose will help him! Let hell chew him up! Why should he call her a whore? Who's been with her? When has she had the time, the place, or the means to sleep with anyone? How is this at all likely? The Moor is being tricked by some crook, some terrible villain, some rotten bastard. Oh, I wish we could unmask scoundrels like that, and give a whip to every good man to beat them senseless with!

IAGO

Keep your voice down.

EMILIA

Oh, to hell with those people! It's the same kind of guy who got you upset and made you suspect I'd cheated on you with the Moor.

IAGO

You're a fool. Shut up.

DESDEMONA

Oh God, Iago, what can I do to win my husband back again? Please go to him, my friend. I swear I have no idea why he stopped loving me. Here I'm kneeling to swear that if I ever did anything to destroy his love for me, either by thoughts or actions, or if I ever took pleasure in anyone else, or if I never did love him, or don't love him now—even though he tries to shake me

165   And ever will—though he do shake me off
To beggarly divorcement—love him dearly,
Comfort forswear me! Unkindness may do much,
And his unkindness may defeat my life,
But never taint my love. I cannot say "whore,"
It does abhor me now I speak the word.
170   To do the act that might the addition earn
Not the world's mass of vanity could make me.

IAGO

I pray you, be content, 'tis but his humor.
The business of the state does him offence,
And he does chide with you.

DESDEMONA

175   If 'twere no other—

IAGO

'Tis but so, I warrant.

Trumpets sound

Hark, how these instruments summon to supper.
The messengers of Venice stays the meat.
Go in, and weep not. All things shall be well.

Exeunt DESDEMONA *and* EMILIA

Enter RODERIGO

180   How now, Roderigo!

RODERIGO

I do not find that thou deal'st justly with me.

IAGO

What in the contrary?

RODERIGO

Every day thou daff'st me with some device, Iago, and
rather, as it seems to me now, keep'st from me all
185.   conveniency than suppliest me with the least advantage of

off—then I hope I have a life of misery! Unkindness is powerful, and his unkindness may kill me, but it'll never destroy my love. I can't say "whore." It makes me sick to say the word even now. I wouldn't do the thing that would make me a whore for all the money in the world.

IAGO

Please calm down. He's just in a bad mood. Political business is bothering him, and he's just taking it out on you.

DESDEMONA

If only that were all it is—

IAGO

It is, I promise.

Trumpets sound.

Those trumpets are calling us in to dinner. The Venetians are waiting for their food. Go in, and don't cry. Everything will be all right.

DESDEMONA *and* EMILIA *exit.*
RODERIGO *enters.*

How are you, Roderigo?

RODERIGO

I don't think you're treating me fairly.

IAGO

What makes you say that?

RODERIGO

Every day you put me off with some trick. Instead of finding opportunities for me, you seem to be preventing me from making any progress. Well, I won't take

hope. I will indeed no longer endure it, nor am I yet
persuaded to put up in peace what already I have foolishly
suffered.

IAGO

Will you hear me, Roderigo?

RODERIGO

190   I have heard too much, and your words and performances
are no kin together.

IAGO

You charge me most unjustly.

RODERIGO

With naught but truth. I have wasted myself out of my
means. The jewels you have had from me to deliver
195   Desdemona would half have corrupted a votaress. You
have told me she hath received them and returned me
expectations and comforts of sudden respect and
acquaintance, but I find none.

IAGO

Well, go to. Very well.

RODERIGO

200   "Very well," "go to"! I cannot go to, man, nor 'tis not very
well. Nay, I think it is scurvy, and begin to find myself
fopped in it.

IAGO

Very well.

RODERIGO

I tell you 'tis not very well. I will make myself known to
205   Desdemona. If she will return me my jewels I will give
over my suit and repent my unlawful solicitation. If not,
assure yourself I will seek satisfaction of you.

IAGO

You have said now.

RODERIGO

Ay, and said nothing but what I protest intendment of
210   doing.

it any longer. And I'm not going to sit back and accept
what you've done.

IAGO

Will you listen to me, Roderigo?

RODERIGO

I've listened to you too much already. Your words and
actions don't match up.

IAGO

That's not fair.

RODERIGO

It's the truth. I've got no money left. The jewels you
took from me to deliver to Desdemona would've made
even a nun want to sleep with me. You told me she got
them, and that she promised to give me a little something in return soon, but nothing like that ever happens.

IAGO

Well, all right then. Fine.

RODERIGO

"Fine!" he says. "All right!" It's not fine, and I'm not
all right! It's wrong, and I'm starting to realize I'm
being cheated!

IAGO

Okay.

RODERIGO

It's not okay! I'm going to tell Desdemona my feelings. If she returns my jewels, I'll stop pursuing her
and apologize to her. If not, I'll challenge you to a
duel.

IAGO

You've said what you have to say now.

RODERIGO

Yes, and I'll do everything I just said.

IAGO

Why, now I see there's mettle in thee, and even from this
instant to build on thee a better opinion than ever before.
Give me thy hand, Roderigo. Thou hast taken against me
a most just exception, but yet I protest I have dealt most
215   directly in thy affair.

RODERIGO

It hath not appeared.

IAGO

I grant indeed it hath not appeared, and your suspicion is
not without wit and judgment. But, Roderigo, if thou hast
that in thee indeed, which I have greater reason to believe
220   now than ever—I mean purpose, courage and valor—this
night show it. If thou the next night following enjoy not
Desdemona, take me from this world with treachery and
devise engines for my life.

RODERIGO

Well, what is it? Is it within reason and compass?

IAGO

225   Sir, there is especial commission come from Venice to
depute Cassio in Othello's place.

RODERIGO

Is that true? Why, then Othello and Desdemona return
again to Venice.

IAGO

Oh, no, he goes into Mauritania and taketh away with him
230   the fair Desdemona, unless his abode be lingered here by
some accident—wherein none can be so determinate as
the removing of Cassio.

RODERIGO

How do you mean, removing of him?

IAGO

Why, by making him uncapable of Othello's place:
235   knocking out his brains.

RODERIGO

And that you would have me to do!

IAGO

Well, all right then. Now I see that you have some guts. From this moment on I have a higher opinion of you than before. Give me your hand, Roderigo. Your complaint against me is perfectly understandable, but I still insist I've done everything I could to help you.

RODERIGO

It doesn't look that way to me.

IAGO

I admit it doesn't look that way to me, and the fact that you suspect me shows that you're smart. But Roderigo, if you're as courageous and determined as I think you are, then wait just a bit longer. If you're not having sex with Desdemona tomorrow night, then I suggest you find some way to stab me in the back and kill me.

RODERIGO

Well, what's your plan? Is it feasible?

IAGO

Venice has made Cassio governor here on Cyprus.

RODERIGO

Is that true? Then Desdemona and Othello will go back to Venice.

IAGO

Oh, no. He'll go to Mauritania and take the beautiful Desdemona with him, unless he gets stuck here for some reason. The best way to extend his stay here is to get rid of Cassio.

RODERIGO

What do you mean, get rid of him?

IAGO

I mean knock his brains out, so he can't take Othello's place.

RODERIGO

And that's what you want me to do!

IAGO
Ay, if you dare do yourself a profit and a right. He sups
tonight with a harlotry, and thither will I go to him. He
knows not yet of his honorable fortune. If you will watch
240   his going thence (which I will fashion to fall out between
twelve and one) you may take him at your pleasure. I will
be near to second your attempt, and he shall fall between
us. Come, stand not amazed at it, but go along with me. I
will show you such a necessity in his death that you shall
245   think yourself bound to put it on him. It is now high
suppertime, and the night grows to waste. About it!

RODERIGO
I will hear further reason for this.

IAGO
And you shall be satisfied.

Exeunt

IAGO

Yes, if you want to help yourself. He's having dinner tonight with a prostitute, and I'll go visit him. He doesn't know he's been appointed governor yet. When you see him walking by here (as I'll make sure he does between twelve and one) you can nab him. I'll be nearby to help you, and between the two of us we can handle him. Come on, don't stand there in a daze. Come along with me. I'll give you such reasons for killing him that you'll feel obliged to snuff him out. It's nearly dinner time, and the night's going to be wasted. Let's go!

RODERIGO

I want to hear more about this.

IAGO

You will. You'll hear all you want to hear.

They exit.

ACT 4, SCENE 3

Enter OTHELLO, LODOVICO, DESDEMONA, EMILIA *and*
attendants

LODOVICO
I do beseech you, sir, trouble yourself no further.

OTHELLO
Oh, pardon me, 'twill do me good to walk.

LODOVICO
Madam, good night. I humbly thank your ladyship.

DESDEMONA
Your honor is most welcome.

OTHELLO
5   Will you walk, sir?—O Desdemona—

DESDEMONA
My lord?

OTHELLO
Get you to bed on th' instant, I will be returned
Forthwith. Dismiss your attendant there, look 't be done.

DESDEMONA
I will, my lord.

Exeunt OTHELLO, LODOVICO, *and attendants*

EMILIA
10   How goes it now? He looks gentler than he did.

DESDEMONA
He says he will return incontinent,
And hath commanded me to go to bed
And bid me to dismiss you.

EMILIA
Dismiss me?

DESDEMONA
It was his bidding. Therefore, good Emilia,
15   Give me my nightly wearing, and adieu.
We must not now displease him.

ACT 4, SCENE 3

OTHELLO, LODOVICO, DESDEMONA *and* EMILIA *enter, with attendants.*

LODOVICO

Please, sir, don't trouble yourself.

OTHELLO

I beg your pardon; walking will make me feel better.

LODOVICO

Good night, madam. Thank you.

DESDEMONA

You're most welcome.

OTHELLO

Would you walk out with me, sir?—Oh, Desdemona—

DESDEMONA

Yes, my lord?

OTHELLO

Go to bed right this minute. I'll be there shortly. Send your maid Emilia away. Make sure you do what I say.

DESDEMONA

I will, my lord.

OTHELLO, LODOVICO, *and attendants exit.*

How are things now? He looks calmer than he did before.

DESDEMONA

He says he'll come back right away. He asked me to go to bed and to send you away.

EMILIA

Send me away?

DESDEMONA

That's what he said. So give me my nightgown, Emilia, and I'll say goodnight. We shouldn't displease him.

EMILIA
Ay. Would you had never seen him!

DESDEMONA
So would not I. My love doth so approve him
That even his stubbornness, his checks, his frowns—
20   Prithee, unpin me—have grace and favor.

EMILIA
I have laid those sheets you bade me on the bed.

DESDEMONA
All's one. Good Father, how foolish are our minds!
If I do die before thee, prithee, shroud me
In one of these same sheets.

EMILIA
                                    Come, come! You talk!

DESDEMONA
25   My mother had a maid called Barbary,
She was in love, and he she loved proved mad
And did forsake her. She had a song of "Willow,"
An old thing 'twas, but it expressed her fortune
And she died singing it. That song tonight
30   Will not go from my mind. I have much to do
But to go hang my head all at one side
And sing it like poor Barbary. Prithee, dispatch.

EMILIA
Shall I go fetch your nightgown?

DESDEMONA
                                    No, unpin me here.
This Lodovico is a proper man.

EMILIA
35   A very handsome man.

DESDEMONA
                        He speaks well.

EMILIA
I know a lady in Venice would have walked barefoot
to Palestine for a touch of his nether lip.

EMILIA

Yes. I wish you'd never met him.

DESDEMONA

That's not what I wish. I love him even when he's harsh and mean—Help me unpin this, would you?—I love even his stubbornness, his frowns, his bad moods.

EMILIA

I put those wedding sheets on your bed, as you asked.

DESDEMONA

It doesn't matter. Oh, how silly we are! If I die before you do make sure I'm wrapped in those sheets in my coffin.

EMILIA

Listen to you! Don't be silly!

DESDEMONA

My mother had a maid named Barbary. She was in love, and her lover turned out to be wild and left her. She knew an old song called "Willow" that reminded her of her own story, and she died singing it. I can't get that song out of my head tonight. It's all I can do to keep myself from hanging my head down in despair and singing it like poor Barbary. Please, hurry up.

EMILIA

Should I get your nightgown?

DESDEMONA

No, just help me unpin this. That Lodovico is a good-looking man.

EMILIA

He's very handsome.

DESDEMONA

He speaks well.

EMILIA

I know a lady in Venice who'd walk all the way to Palestine for a kiss from him.

DESDEMONA
(singing)

> The poor soul sat sighing by a sycamore tree,
> Sing all a green willow.
40   Her hand on her bosom, her head on her knee,
> Sing willow, willow, willow.
> The fresh streams ran by her, and murmured her moans,
> Sing willow, willow, willow.
> Her salt tears fell from her, and softened the stones
45   Sing willow, willow, willow—
> Lay by these—
>   Willow, willow—
> Prithee, hie thee, he'll come anon—
> Sing all a green willow must be my garland.
> Let nobody blame him, his scorn I approve—

50   Nay, that's not next—Hark! Who is 't that knocks?

EMILIA
It's the wind.

DESDEMONA
(sings)

> I called my love false love but what said he then?
>   Sing willow, willow, willow.

If I court more women you'll couch with more men—
So, get thee gone, good night. Mine eyes do itch,
55   Doth that bode weeping?

EMILIA
                     'Tis neither here nor there.

DESDEMONA
I have heard it said so. Oh, these men, these men!
Dost thou in conscience think—tell me, Emilia—
That there be women do abuse their husbands
In such gross kind?

EMILIA
                 There be some such, no question.

DESDEMONA
60   Wouldst thou do such a deed for all the world?

DESDEMONA

> *(singing)*
> *The poor soul sat singing by the sycamore tree,*
> *Everyone sing the green willow,*
> *She had her hand on her breast and her head on her knee,*
> *Sing willow, willow, willow.*
> *The fresh streams ran by her and murmured her moans,*
> *Sing willow, willow, willow.*
> *Her salt tears fell from her and softened the stones,*
> *Sing willow, willow, willow.—*
> *Put these things over there.—*
> *Please, hurry, he'll come right away.—*
> *Everyone sing, a green willow must be my garland.*
> *Nobody blame him, he's right to hate me—*
> No, that's not how it goes.—Who's knocking?

EMILIA

> It's the wind.

DESDEMONA

> *(singing) I told my lover he didn't love me, but what did*
> *he say? Sing willow, willow, willow.*
> If I chase more women, you'll sleep with more men—
> Okay, go away now. Good night. My eyes itch—is
> that an omen I'll be crying soon?

EMILIA

> No, it doesn't mean anything.

DESDEMONA

> I heard someone say that's what it means. Oh, these
> men, these men! Do you honestly think—tell me,
> Emilia—there are women who'd cheat on their hus-
> bands in such a disgusting manner?

EMILIA

> There are women like that out there, no question.

DESDEMONA

> Would you ever do such a thing for all the world?

EMILIA
> Why, would not you?

DESDEMONA
>   No, by this heavenly light!

EMILIA
> Nor I neither, by this heavenly light.
> I might do 't as well i' th' dark.

DESDEMONA
> Wouldst thou do such a deed for all the world?

EMILIA
65 The world's a huge thing. It is a great price for a small vice.

DESDEMONA
> In troth, I think thou wouldst not.

EMILIA
> In troth, I think I should, and undo 't when I had done.
> Marry, I would not do such a thing for a joint-ring, nor for
> measures of lawn, nor for gowns, petticoats, nor caps, nor
70 any petty exhibition. But for the whole world? Why, who
> would not make her husband a cuckold to make him a
> monarch? I should venture purgatory for 't.

DESDEMONA
> Beshrew me, if I would do such a wrong
> For the whole world.

EMILIA
75 Why the wrong is but a wrong i' th' world, and having the
> world for your labor, 'tis a wrong in your own world, and
> you might quickly make it right.

DESDEMONA
> I do not think there is any such woman.

EMILIA
> Yes, a dozen, and as many to th' vantage as would store the
80 world they played for.
> But I do think it is their husbands' faults
> If wives do fall. Say that they slack their duties
> And pour our treasures into foreign laps,
> Or else break out in peevish jealousies,

EMILIA

Why, wouldn't you?

DESDEMONA

By the light of heaven, no, I would not!

EMILIA

I wouldn't either, by daylight. It would be easier to do it in the dark.

DESDEMONA

Could you really do such a thing, for all the world?

EMILIA

The world's huge. It's a big prize for such a small sin.

DESDEMONA

I don't think you would.

EMILIA

Actually I think I would, and then I'd undo it after I did it. I wouldn't do it for a nice ring, or fine linen, or pretty gowns or petticoats or hats. But for the whole world? Who wouldn't cheat on her husband to make him king? I'd risk my soul for that.

DESDEMONA

I'd never do such a bad thing, not for the whole world!

EMILIA

Why, a bad action is just a wrong in this world, but when you've won the whole world, it's a wrong in your own world, so you can make it right then.

DESDEMONA

I don't think any woman like that exists.

EMILIA

Yes, a dozen of them—as many as there are women in the world, in fact. But I do think it's the husband's fault if we wives cheat on them. For instance, our husbands may stop sleeping with us, and give it out to other women instead. Or they may get insanely jeal-

85 Throwing restraint upon us. Or say they strike us,
Or scant our former having in despite.
Why, we have galls, and though we have some grace,
Yet have we some revenge. Let husbands know
Their wives have sense like them. They see and smell
90 And have their palates both for sweet and sour,
As husbands have. What is it that they do
When they change us for others? Is it sport?
I think it is. And doth affection breed it?
I think it doth. Is 't frailty that thus errs?
95 It is so too. And have not we affections,
Desires for sport, and frailty, as men have?
Then let them use us well, else let them know,
The ills we do, their ills instruct us so.

DESDEMONA
Good night, good night. Heaven me such uses send,
100 Not to pick bad from bad, but by bad mend!

Exeunt

ous, and keep us from going anywhere. Or let's say
they hit us, or cut back on the money they give us out
of spite. We have feelings. We may be able to forgive
them, but we want to get back at them too. Husbands
need to know that their wives are human beings too.
They see, smell, and taste sweet and sour just like their
husbands. Why do they replace us with other women?
Do they do it for fun? I think they do. Is it out of lust?
I think so. Is it a weakness? It is. And don't we have
passions, and a taste for fun, and weaknesses, just like
men? Then tell them to treat us well. Or let them figure out that the bad things we do are just what we
learned from them.

DESDEMONA

Good night, good night. I pray that God will let me
learn from women like that—not to follow their bad
example, but to avoid it!

They exit.

ACT FIVE

SCENE 1

Enter IAGO *and* RODERIGO

IAGO

    Here, stand behind this bulk, straight will he come.
    Wear thy good rapier bare, and put it home.
    Quick, quick! Fear nothing. I'll be at thy elbow.
    It makes us, or it mars us. Think on that,
5   And fix most firm thy resolution.

RODERIGO

    Be near at hand, I may miscarry in 't.

IAGO

    Here, at thy hand. Be bold, and take thy stand.

Withdraws

RODERIGO

    I have no great devotion to the deed
    And yet he hath given me satisfying reasons.
10   'Tis but a man gone. Forth, my sword: he dies.

IAGO

    (aside) I have rubbed this young quat almost to the sense,
    And he grows angry. Now, whether he kill Cassio
    Or Cassio him, or each do kill the other,
    Every way makes my gain. Live Roderigo,
15   He calls me to a restitution large
    Of gold and jewels that I bobbed from him
    As gifts to Desdemona.
    It must not be. If Cassio do remain
    He hath a daily beauty in his life
20   That makes me ugly. And besides, the Moor
    May unfold me to him—there stand I in much peril.
    No, he must die. But so, I hear him coming.

ACT FIVE

SCENE 1

IAGO *and* RODERIGO *enter.*

IAGO

Here, stand behind this wall; he'll come right away. Keep your sword out, and then stick it in as far as it'll go. Quick, quick. Don't be afraid. I'll be right next to you. This will either make us or break us. Keep that in mind, and be steady.

RODERIGO

Stay right near me. I may mess it up.

IAGO

I'm right behind you. Be bold, and get ready.

IAGO *moves aside.*

RODERIGO

I don't really want to do this, but he's given me good reasons. I guess it's only one man—no big deal. My sword comes out, and he dies.

IAGO

(to himself) I've rubbed this young pimple until he's ready to pop, and now he's angry. Whether he kills Cassio, or Cassio kills him, or they kill each other, it all works in my favor. If Roderigo survives, though, he'll ask me for all the gold and jewelry that I stole from him and said I gave to Desdemona. I can't let that happen. If Cassio survives, he's so handsome and well-spoken that he makes me look ugly. And besides, the Moor might tell him about my lies about him.—That would be very dangerous for me. No, he's got to die. Let it be so. I hear him coming.

Enter CASSIO

RODERIGO
I know his gait, 'tis he.—Villain, thou diest!

Thrusts at CASSIO

CASSIO
That thrust had been mine enemy indeed
25 But that my coat is better than thou know'st
I will make proof of thine.

Draws, and wounds RODERIGO

RODERIGO
Oh, I am slain!

IAGO *from behind wounds* CASSIO *in the legs, exits*

CASSIO
I am maimed for ever. Help, ho! Murder! Murder!

Enter OTHELLO

OTHELLO
The voice of Cassio. Iago keeps his word.

RODERIGO
Oh, villain that I am!

OTHELLO
30 It is even so.

CASSIO
Oh, help, ho! Light! A surgeon!

OTHELLO
'Tis he. Oh, brave Iago, honest and just,
That hast such noble sense of thy friend's wrong!

CASSIO *enters.*

RODERIGO

I know the sound of his walk.—Die, villain!

RODERIGO *thrusts his sword at* CASSIO.

CASSIO

That thrust might really have hurt me if I didn't have this armor on under my cloak. Now let's see what you've got on.

CASSIO *draws his sword and stabs* RODERIGO.

RODERIGO

Oh, I'm dead!

> *From behind,* IAGO *stabs* CASSIO *in the leg and then exits.*

CASSIO

I'll be crippled forever! Help! Murder! murder!

OTHELLO *enters.*

OTHELLO

That's Cassio's voice. Iago has kept his word.

RODERIGO

Oh, what a villain I am!

OTHELLO

That's the truth.

CASSIO

Help me! Get some light! Get me a surgeon!

OTHELLO

It's him! Brave Iago, how honest and trustworthy you are! You even went as far as murder to help your friend in his misfortune. You teach me how I should act.

Thou teachest me. Minion, your dear lies dead,
35   And your unblest fate hies. Strumpet, I come.
For, of my heart, those charms, thine eyes, are blotted.
Thy bed, lust-stained, shall with lust's blood be spotted.

Exit

Enter LODOVICO *and* GRATIANO

CASSIO
What, ho! No watch? No passage? Murder! Murder!

GRATIANO
40   'Tis some mischance, the cry is very direful.

CASSIO
Oh, help!

LODOVICO
Hark!

RODERIGO
Oh, wretched villain!

LODOVICO
Two or three groan. 'Tis heavy night,
45   These may be counterfeits. Let's think 't unsafe
To come in to the cry without more help.

RODERIGO
Nobody come? Then shall I bleed to death.

LODOVICO
Hark!

Enter IAGO

GRATIANO
Here's one comes in his shirt, with light and weapons.

IAGO
50   Who's there? Whose noise is this that ones on murder?

Whore, your lover's dead now, and you'll be going to hell soon. I'm coming, slut! I've shut the memory of your beautiful eyes out of my heart. You've already stained our sheets with your lust; now I'll stain them with your whore's blood.

OTHELLO *exits.*

LODOVICO *and* GRATIANO *enter.*

CASSIO

Help! Isn't there a guard around? No one passing by? Murder! Murder!

GRATIANO

Something's wrong, the man sounds panicked.

CASSIO

Oh, help!

LODOVICO

Listen!

RODERIGO

I've acted like such a villain!

LODOVICO

Two or three men are groaning. But it's dark out, and it could be a trap. It's not safe to go near them till we get more help.

RODERIGO

Nobody's coming? I'll bleed to death.

LODOVICO

Look!

IAGO *enters.*

GRATIANO

Here's someone coming in his pajamas, with a candle and weapons.

IAGO

Who's there? Who's shouting "murder"?

LODOVICO
> We do not know.

IAGO
>   Do not you hear a cry?

CASSIO
> Here, here! For heaven's sake, help me!

IAGO
>   What's the matter?

GRATIANO
> *(to* LODOVICO*)* This is Othello's ancient, as I take it.

LODOVICO
> The same indeed, a very valiant fellow.

IAGO
55 > *(to* CASSIO*)* What are you here that cry so grievously?

CASSIO
> Iago? Oh, I am spoiled, undone by villains!
> Give me some help.

IAGO
> Oh, me, lieutenant! What villains have done this?

CASSIO
> I think that one of them is hereabout,
60 > And cannot make away.

IAGO
>   Oh, treacherous villains!—
> *(to* LODOVICO *and* GRATIANO*)*
> What are you there? Come in, and give some help.

RODERIGO
> Oh, help me there!

CASSIO
> That's one of them.

IAGO
>   O murd'rous slave! O villain!

Stabs RODERIGO

LODOVICO

We don't know.

IAGO

Didn't you hear someone shouting?

CASSIO

I'm here, here! For heaven's sake, help me!

IAGO

What's the matter?

GRATIANO

(to LODOVICO*)* That's Othello's ensign, I think.

LODOVICO

It is. He's a good man.

IAGO

(to CASSIO*)* Who's shouting so loudly?

CASSIO

Is that you, Iago? I'm here, I've been destroyed by villains! Help me.

IAGO

Oh, lieutenant! What villains did this to you?

CASSIO

I think one of them is nearby and can't get away.

IAGO

The treacherous criminals!—*(to* LODOVICO *and* GRATIANO*)* Who's there? Come here and help!

RODERIGO

Somebody help me over here!

CASSIO

That's one of them.

IAGO

(to RODERIGO*)* Murderer! Villain!

IAGO *stabs* RODERIGO.

RODERIGO
> O damned Iago! O inhuman dog!

IAGO
65 > Kill men i' th' dark! Where be these bloody thieves?
> How silent is this town!—Ho! murder! murder!—
> What may you be? Are you of good or evil?

LODOVICO
> As you shall prove us, praise us.

IAGO
> Signior Lodovico?

LODOVICO
70 > He, sir.

IAGO
> I cry you mercy. Here's Cassio hurt by villains.

GRATIANO
> Cassio!

IAGO
> How is 't, brother!

CASSIO
> My leg is cut in two.

IAGO
75 > Marry, heaven forbid!
> Light, gentlemen, I'll bind it with my shirt.

Enter BIANCA

BIANCA
> What is the matter, ho? Who is 't that cried?

IAGO
> Who is 't that cried?

BIANCA
>   Oh, my dear Cassio!
> My sweet Cassio! O Cassio, Cassio, Cassio!

IAGO
80 > O notable strumpet! Cassio, may you suspect
> Who they should be that have thus mangled you?

RODERIGO

Damned Iago! You inhuman dog!

IAGO

Killing men in the dark? Where are these murderers? This is such a quiet, sleepy town!—Murder, murder!—Who's that coming? Are you good or evil?

LODOVICO

Judge for yourself.

IAGO

Signor Lodovico?

LODOVICO

That's me.

IAGO

I beg your pardon. Cassio's been wounded.

GRATIANO

Cassio!

IAGO

How are you doing, brother?

CASSIO

My leg's been cut in two.

IAGO

God forbid! Bring me some light, gentlemen, I'll bind the wound with my shirt.

BIANCA *enters.*

BIANCA

What's the matter? Who's shouting?

IAGO

Who's shouting?

BIANCA

Oh, my dear Cassio! My sweet Cassio! Oh, Cassio, Cassio, Cassio!

IAGO

You notorious whore! Cassio, do you know who might have stabbed you like this?

CASSIO
No.

GRATIANO
I am sorry to find you thus. I have been to seek you.

IAGO
Lend me a garter. So.—Oh, for a chair,
85   To bear him easily hence!

BIANCA
Alas, he faints! O Cassio, Cassio, Cassio!

IAGO
Gentlemen all, I do suspect this trash
To be a party in this injury.—
Patience awhile, good Cassio.—Come, come,
90   Lend me a light. Know we this face or no?
Alas, my friend and my dear countryman
Roderigo! No—yes, sure! Yes, 'tis Roderigo.

GRATIANO
What, of Venice?

IAGO
Even he, sir. Did you know him?

GRATIANO
95   Know him? Ay.

IAGO
Signior Gratiano? I cry you gentle pardon,
These bloody accidents must excuse my manners
That so neglected you.

GRATIANO
                                    I am glad to see you.

IAGO
How do you, Cassio?—Oh, a chair, a chair!

GRATIANO
100   Roderigo!

IAGO
He, he, 'tis he.

A chair is brought in

CASSIO

No.

GRATIANO

I'm sorry to find you like this. I've been looking all over for you.

IAGO

Lend me your sash—Oh, if we only had a stretcher to carry him out of here!

BIANCA

He's fainted! Oh Cassio, Cassio, Cassio!

IAGO

Sir, I believe this piece of trash, Bianca, has something to do with all this trouble.—Hang in there, Cassio.—Come here, bring the light. Do you recognize this face? Oh, no, it's my friend and countryman, Roderigo.—Yes, it's Roderigo!

GRATIANO

What, Roderigo from Venice?

IAGO

That's the one, sir. Do you know him?

GRATIANO

Know him? Yes.

IAGO

Signor Gratiano, I beg your pardon. I didn't mean to ignore you—it's just because of this bloody uproar.

GRATIANO

I'm glad to see you.

IAGO

How are you doing, Cassio?—Someone bring me a stretcher!

GRATIANO

Roderigo!

IAGO

It's him, it's him.

A stretcher is brought in.

Oh, that's well said—the chair!
Some good man bear him carefully from hence.
I'll fetch the general's surgeon.—*(to* BIANCA*)* For you,
    mistress,
Save you your labor.—He that lies slain here, Cassio,
105 Was my dear friend. What malice was between you?

CASSIO

None in the world, nor do I know the man.

IAGO

(to BIANCA*)*
What, look you pale?—Oh, bear him out o' the air.—

CASSIO *and* RODERIGO *are borne off*

Do you perceive the gastness of her eye?—Stay you, good
gentlemen.—Look you pale, mistress?—
110 Nay, if you stare, we shall hear more anon.—
Behold her well. I pray you, look upon her.
Do you see, gentlemen? Nay, guiltiness
Will speak, though tongues were out of use.

Enter EMILIA

EMILIA

Alas, what is the matter? What is the matter, husband?

IAGO

115 Cassio hath here been set on in the dark
By Roderigo and fellows that are 'scaped.
He's almost slain, and Roderigo dead.

EMILIA

Alas, good gentleman! Alas, good Cassio!

IAGO

This is the fruits of whoring. Prithee, Emilia,
120 Go know of Cassio where he supped tonight.—
(to BIANCA*)* What, do you shake at that?

Good—here's the stretcher. Get somebody strong to carry him out of here. I'll get the general's surgeon. *(to* BIANCA*)* As for you, ma'am, don't bother. The man lying here was my dear friend, Roderigo. —What was the problem between you?

CASSIO

There wasn't any problem. I don't even know him.

IAGO

(to BIANCA*)* You're pale?—Get Cassio out of here.— You look awfully pale, Bianca.

CASSIO *and* RODERIGO *are carried away.*

Do you see how afraid she is? Watch her, we'll get the whole story. Keep an eye on her. Do you see? The guilty speak volumes even when they're silent.

EMILIA *enters.*

EMILIA

What's the matter? What's the matter, husband?

IAGO

Cassio was attacked here in the dark by Roderigo and men who escaped. He's near death, and Roderigo's dead already.

EMILIA

Oh, no, good gentleman! Oh no, good Cassio!

IAGO

This is what happens when you visit whores. Please, Emilia, ask Cassio where he was at dinner tonight.— *(to* BIANCA*)* What, does that make you nervous?

BIANCA

> He supped at my house, but I therefore shake not.

IAGO

> Oh, did he so? I charge you, go with me.

EMILIA

> Oh, fie upon thee, strumpet!

BIANCA

125 > I am no strumpet, but of life as honest
> As you that thus abuse me.

EMILIA

> As I! Fie upon thee!

IAGO

> Kind gentlemen, let's go see poor Cassio dressed.—
> Come, mistress, you must tell 's another tale.
> Emilia, run you to the citadel
130 > And tell my lord and lady what hath happed.—
> Will you go on afore?
> *(aside)*
> This is the night
> That either makes me or fordoes me quite.

Exeunt

BIANCA

He ate at my house, but that doesn't make me nervous.

IAGO

Oh, did he? I order you to come with me.

EMILIA

Go to hell, you whore!

BIANCA

I'm no whore. I'm as moral as you are.

EMILIA

As moral as me! Damn you!

IAGO

Gentlemen, let's go make sure Cassio's wounds are properly dressed.—Come on, ma'am, you can tell us another story. Emilia, go to the castle and tell Othello and Desdemona what happened.—Will you please go now? *(to himself)* This is the night that'll either make me or break me.

They all exit.

ACT 5, SCENE 2

DESDEMONA *asleep in bed*
Enter OTHELLO *with a light*

OTHELLO
It is the cause, it is the cause, my soul.
Let me not name it to you, you chaste stars,
It is the cause. Yet I'll not shed her blood,
Nor scar that whiter skin of hers than snow
5   And smooth as monumental alabaster.
Yet she must die, else she'll betray more men.
Put out the light, and then put out the light.
If I quench thee, thou flaming minister,
I can again thy former light restore
10   Should I repent me. But once put out thy light,
Thou cunning'st pattern of excelling nature,
I know not where is that Promethean heat
That can thy light relume. When I have plucked thy rose
I cannot give it vital growth again,
15   It must needs wither. I'll smell thee on the tree.
Oh, balmy breath, that dost almost persuade
Justice to break her sword! One more, one more.
Be thus when thou art dead and I will kill thee
And love thee after. *(kissing her)* One more, and that's
            the last.
20   So sweet was ne'er so fatal. I must weep,
But they are cruel tears. This sorrow's heavenly,
It strikes where it doth love. She wakes.

DESDEMONA
Who's there? Othello?

OTHELLO
Ay, Desdemona.

ACT 5, SCENE 2

DESDEMONA *is asleep in bed.* OTHELLO *enters with a candle.*

OTHELLO

I have to do it, I have to do it. I have to keep my reason in mind. I won't say out loud what my reason is, but I have to do it. But I won't shed any of her blood or scar that beautiful skin, whiter than snow and smooth as the finest marble. But she's got to die, or she'll cheat on other men. Put out the light of the candle, and then put out the light of her heart. If I extinguish the candle, I can light it again if I regret it. But once I kill you, you beautiful, fake woman, I do not know the magic that could bring you back. When I've plucked this rose, I can't make it grow again; it will have no choice but to wither and die. Let me smell you while you're still on the tree. *(he kisses her)* Oh, that sweet breath almost convinces me not to kill you and carry out justice. One more, one more kiss. If you're this beautiful when you're dead, I'll kill you and then love you afterward. *(kissing her)* One more, and this is the last. Such a sweet kiss was never so deadly. I have to cry, but I have to be cruel too. I'm acting like God in the Old Testament—I have to punish the one I love. She's waking up.

DESDEMONA

Who's there? Othello?

OTHELLO

Yes, Desdemona.

DESDEMONA

25   Will you come to bed, my lord?

OTHELLO

Have you prayed tonight, Desdemon?

DESDEMONA

Ay, my lord.

OTHELLO

If you bethink yourself of any crime
Unreconciled as yet to heaven and grace,
30   Solicit for it straight.

DESDEMONA

Alack, my lord, what do you mean by that?

OTHELLO

Well, do it, and be brief. I will walk by.
I would not kill thy unpreparèd spirit.
No, heavens forfend, I would not kill thy soul!

DESDEMONA

35   Talk you of killing?

OTHELLO

                              Ay, I do.

DESDEMONA

                                                        Then heaven
Have mercy on me!

OTHELLO

Amen, with all my heart.

DESDEMONA

If you say, I hope you will not kill me.

OTHELLO

Humh!

DESDEMONA

40   And yet I fear you, for you're fatal then
When your eyes roll so. Why I should fear I know not,
Since guiltiness I know not. But yet I feel I fear.

OTHELLO

Think on thy sins.

DESDEMONA

Will you come to bed, my lord?

OTHELLO

Have you said your prayers tonight, Desdemona?

DESDEMONA

Yes, my lord.

OTHELLO

If you can think of any crime you haven't confessed, then pray for forgiveness right away.

DESDEMONA

Oh, my lord, what do you mean by that?

OTHELLO

Well, hurry up and confess. Be quick about it. I'll wait over here. I don't want to kill you before you've readied your soul. No, I don't want to send your soul to hell when I kill you.

DESDEMONA

You're talking about killing?

OTHELLO

Yes, I am.

DESDEMONA

Then heaven have mercy on me.

OTHELLO

Amen to that, from the bottom of my heart.

DESDEMONA

If you really feel that way, then I hope you won't kill me.

OTHELLO

Hmmph!

DESDEMONA

You're scaring me. You terrify me when you have that look in your eyes. I don't know why I should be afraid, since I haven't done anything wrong. But I'm still afraid.

OTHELLO

Think of your sins.

DESDEMONA
They are loves I bear to you.

OTHELLO
45   Ay, and for that thou diest.

DESDEMONA
That death's unnatural that kills for loving.
Alas, why gnaw you so your nether lip?
Some bloody passion shakes your very frame.
These are portents, but yet I hope, I hope
50   They do not point on me.

OTHELLO
Peace, and be still.

DESDEMONA
I will so. What's the matter?

OTHELLO
That handkerchief
Which I so loved and gave thee, thou gav'st
To Cassio.

DESDEMONA
55   No, by my life and soul!
Send for the man and ask him.

OTHELLO
Sweet soul, take heed, take heed of perjury.
Thou art on thy deathbed.

DESDEMONA
Ay—but not yet to die!

OTHELLO
60   Presently.
Therefore confess thee freely of thy sin,
For to deny each article with oath
Cannot remove nor choke the strong conception
That I do groan withal. Thou art to die.

DESDEMONA
65   Oh, heaven have mercy on me!

OTHELLO
I say "amen."

DESDEMONA

My only sin was loving you too much.

OTHELLO

Yes, that's why you have to die.

DESDEMONA

You're wrong to kill me for loving you. Why are you chewing on your lower lip like that? You're shaking with emotion. These are bad omens, but I hope, I hope, they don't predict my future.

OTHELLO

Quiet. Stay still.

DESDEMONA

I will. What's this all about?

OTHELLO

You gave that handkerchief, the one I loved and gave to you, to Cassio.

DESDEMONA

No, I swear by my life and soul! Bring him here and ask him.

OTHELLO

My sweet darling, don't lie. You're on your deathbed.

DESDEMONA

I am? But I'm not dying yet!

OTHELLO

Yes, right now. So confess your sin freely now. Even if you swear you're innocent of every accusation, you won't change my mind or remove the thought that's tormenting me. You're going to die.

DESDEMONA

Then heaven have mercy on me!

OTHELLO

Amen to that.

DESDEMONA
And have you mercy too! I never did
Offend you in my life, never loved Cassio
But with such general warranty of heaven
As I might love. I never gave him token.

OTHELLO
70 By heaven, I saw my handkerchief in 's hand.
O perjured woman, thou dost stone my heart,
And mak'st me call what I intend to do
A murder, which I thought a sacrifice!
I saw the handkerchief.

DESDEMONA
                                    He found it then,
75 I never gave it him. Send for him hither,
Let him confess a truth.

OTHELLO
                                    He hath confessed.

DESDEMONA
What, my lord?

OTHELLO
                          That he hath usèd thee.

DESDEMONA
How? Unlawfully?

OTHELLO
Ay.

DESDEMONA
80 He will not say so.

OTHELLO
No, his mouth is stopped. Honest Iago
Hath ta'en order for 't.

DESDEMONA
Oh! My fear interprets. What, is he dead?

OTHELLO
Had all his hairs been lives
85 My great revenge had stomach for them all.

DESDEMONA

And you have mercy on me too! I never did anything wrong to you in my life. I never loved Cassio, except with the pure love that I feel for humankind. I never gave him any token of romantic love.

OTHELLO

I saw him holding the handkerchief! You liar, you're turning my heart to stone, and making me call what I'll do murder, when I had been thinking of it as a sacrifice! I saw the handkerchief.

DESDEMONA

He found it somewhere, then. I never gave it to him. Tell him to come here. He'll tell the truth.

OTHELLO

He's already done so.

DESDEMONA

What, my lord?

OTHELLO

That he had sex with you.

DESDEMONA

What? Had sex with me?

OTHELLO

Yes.

DESDEMONA

He wouldn't say that.

OTHELLO

No. He won't say anything anymore. Honest Iago's arranged that.

DESDEMONA

Oh, I'm scared. What, is he dead?

OTHELLO

If he had as many lives as he's got hairs on his head, I would've killed them all in revenge.

DESDEMONA
Alas, he is betrayed and I undone.

OTHELLO
Out, strumpet! weep'st thou for him to my face?

DESDEMONA
Oh, banish me, my lord, but kill me not!

OTHELLO
Down, strumpet!

DESDEMONA
90   Kill me tomorrow—let me live tonight!

OTHELLO
Nay, if you strive—

DESDEMONA
But half an hour!

OTHELLO
Being done, there is no pause.

DESDEMONA
But while I say one prayer!

OTHELLO
95   It is too late. *(he smothers her)*

EMILIA
(within) My lord , my lord! What, ho! My lord, my lord!

OTHELLO
What noise is this?—Not dead? Not yet quite dead?
I that am cruel am yet merciful,
I would not have thee linger in thy pain.
100   So, so.

EMILIA
(within) What, ho! My lord, my lord!

OTHELLO
                                    Who's there?

EMILIA
(within) O good my lord, I would speak a word with you!

DESDEMONA

Oh, he's been betrayed, and I've been ruined.

OTHELLO

What, you whore, are you crying for him right in front of me?

DESDEMONA

Send me away, my lord, but don't kill me!

OTHELLO

Down, whore!

Othello probably wrestles her down.

DESDEMONA

Kill me tomorrow—but let me live tonight.

OTHELLO

No, if you struggle with me—

DESDEMONA

Just half an hour!

OTHELLO

While I'm doing this, I can't pause for a moment.

DESDEMONA

Just let me say one prayer!

OTHELLO

It's too late. *(he smothers her)*

EMILIA

(offstage) My lord, my lord! Hello! My lord, my lord!

OTHELLO

What's that noise? Aren't you dead yet? I know I'm cruel, but I'm merciful too. I don't want you to linger in pain.

EMILIA

(offstage) Hello! My lord, my lord!

OTHELLO

Who's there?

EMILIA

(offstage) Oh my lord, I need to speak to you!

OTHELLO
Yes, 'tis Emilia.—*(to* EMILIA*)* By and by.—She's dead.—
105   'Tis like she comes to speak of Cassio's death,
The noise was high. Ha! No more moving?
Still as the grave. Shall she come in? Were 't good?
I think she stirs again—No. What's best to do?
If she come in, she'll sure speak to my wife—
110   My wife! my wife! what wife? I have no wife.
Oh, insupportable! Oh, heavy hour!
Methinks it should be now a huge eclipse
Of sun and moon, and that th' affrighted globe
Should yawn at alteration.

EMILIA
(within)

                  I do beseech you
115   That I may speak with you, O good my lord!

OTHELLO
I had forgot thee—Oh, come in, Emilia.
Soft, by and by. Let me the curtains draw.
Where art thou?

Unlocks the door. Enter EMILIA

                  What's the matter with thee now?

EMILIA
O my good lord, yonder's foul murders done!

OTHELLO
120   What, now?

EMILIA
But now, my lord.

OTHELLO
It is the very error of the moon,
She comes more nearer earth than she was wont
And makes men mad.

EMILIA
125   Cassio, my lord, hath killed a young Venetian
Called Roderigo.

OTHELLO

Yes, it's Emilia. *(to* EMILIA*)*—Just a minute!—She's dead now.—Emilia's probably come to tell me that Cassio's been killed. The fight outside was loud. So! You're not moving anymore? No, you're as still as a grave. Should I let her in? Is that a good idea? I think she's moving again—No. What should I do? If she comes in, she'll try to speak to my wife. My wife, my wife! What wife? I don't have a wife. Oh, this is unbearable! Oh, the horror! There should be a huge eclipse of the sun and the moon, now that Desdemona's no longer on this earth.

EMILIA

(offstage) Please, my lord. I need to speak with you. Oh, my good lord!

OTHELLO

I'd forgotten about you—Emilia, wait a moment, let me draw the curtains. *(closes the bed curtains)* Where are you? *(unlocks the door)*

EMILIA *enters.*

What's the matter with you now?

EMILIA

Oh, my lord, terrible murders have been committed over there!

OTHELLO

What? Just now?

EMILIA

Yes, just now, my lord.

OTHELLO

It's because of the full moon. It comes too close to the earth and drives men crazy.

EMILIA

Cassio's killed a young Venetian named Roderigo.

OTHELLO

Roderigo killed? And Cassio killed!

EMILIA

No, Cassio is not killed.

OTHELLO

Not Cassio killed! Then murder's out of tune,
And sweet revenge grows harsh.

DESDEMONA

130　　Oh, falsely, falsely murdered!

EMILIA

Alas, what cry is that?

OTHELLO

That? What?

EMILIA

Out and alas, that was my lady's voice.

Opens the bedcurtains

Help! Help, ho, help! O lady, speak again!
135　　Sweet Desdemona! O sweet mistress, speak!

DESDEMONA

A guiltless death I die.

EMILIA

Oh, who hath done this deed?

DESDEMONA

Nobody. I myself. Farewell.
Commend me to my kind lord. Oh, farewell!

Dies

OTHELLO

140　　Why, how should she be murdered?

EMILIA

Alas, who knows?

OTHELLO

You heard her say herself it was not I.

OTHELLO

Roderigo's been killed? And Cassio's killed?

EMILIA

No, Cassio wasn't killed.

OTHELLO

Cassio's not dead? Then the wrong man is dead, and sweet revenge has gone wrong.

DESDEMONA

Oh, I've been murdered unfairly!

EMILIA

Oh Lord, who's that crying?

OTHELLO

That? What?

EMILIA

Oh, no, that was my lady's voice.

EMILIA *opens the bedcurtains.*

Help! Help! Oh, lady, speak again.
Sweet Desdemona! Oh sweet mistress, speak!

DESDEMONA

I'm dying an innocent woman.

EMILIA

Oh, who did this thing?

DESDEMONA

No one. I did it myself. Give my love to my kind husband. Oh, goodbye!

DESDEMONA *dies.*

OTHELLO

Why, how could she have been murdered?

EMILIA

My God, who knows?

OTHELLO

You heard her say it wasn't me.

EMILIA
> She said so. I must needs report the truth.

OTHELLO
> She's like a liar gone to burning hell.
> 'Twas I that killed her.

EMILIA
145 > Oh, the more angel she,
> And you the blacker devil!

OTHELLO
> She turned to folly, and she was a whore.

EMILIA
> Thou dost belie her, and thou art a devil.

OTHELLO
> She was false as water.

EMILIA
>   Thou art rash as fire,
150 > To say that she was false. Oh, she was heavenly true!

OTHELLO
> Cassio did top her, ask thy husband else.
> Oh, I were damned beneath all depth in hell,
> But that I did proceed upon just grounds
> To this extremity. Thy husband knew it all.

EMILIA
155 > My husband!

OTHELLO
>   Thy husband.

EMILIA
>   That she was false to wedlock?

OTHELLO
> Ay, with Cassio. Had she been true,
> If heaven would make me such another world

> Of one entire and perfect chrysolite,
> I'd not have sold her for it.

EMILIA
>   My husband?

EMILIA

Yes, she said that. I must go report what happened.

OTHELLO

She was lying even as she was going down to hell. I did kill her.

EMILIA

Then she was even more an angel, and you're an even blacker devil!

OTHELLO

She cheated on me, and she was a whore.

EMILIA

You slander her, you devil.

OTHELLO

She was fickle and unfaithful, like water.

EMILIA

You've lost your mind to accuse her of cheating. She was utterly true to you!

OTHELLO

Cassio had sex with her. Ask your husband if you doubt me. If I didn't have a good reason to do this, damn me to the very bottom of hell. Your husband knew about everything.

EMILIA

My husband!

OTHELLO

Your husband.

EMILIA

He said she was unfaithful?

OTHELLO

Yes, with Cassio. If she'd been faithful to me, I never would have given her up, not even if God himself offered me a jewel as big as a planet in exchange for her.

EMILIA

My husband.

OTHELLO

160   Ay, 'twas he that told me on her first.
An honest man he is, and hates the slime
That sticks on filthy deeds.

EMILIA

                        My husband!

OTHELLO

What needs this iterance, woman? I say thy husband.

EMILIA

O mistress, villainy hath made mocks with love!
165   My husband say that she was false!

OTHELLO

                        He, woman.
I say "thy husband"—dost understand the word?
My friend, thy husband, honest, honest Iago.

EMILIA

If he say so, may his pernicious soul
Rot half a grain a day! He lies to th' heart.
170   She was too fond of her most filthy bargain.

    OTHELLO *draws his sword*

OTHELLO
    Ha!

EMILIA

Do thy worst.
This deed of thine is no more worthy heaven
Than thou wast worthy her.

OTHELLO

                  Peace, you were best.

EMILIA

175   Thou hast not half that power to do me harm
As I have to be hurt. O gull! O dolt!
As ignorant as dirt! Thou hast done a deed—
I care not for thy sword, I'll make thee known

OTHELLO

Yes, he's the one who first told me about her. He's an honest man who detests evil actions.

EMILIA

My husband?

OTHELLO

Why do you keep repeating that, woman? I'm telling you, your husband.

EMILIA

Oh, my mistress, a villain has made a mockery of your love! My husband said she was unfaithful!

OTHELLO

Yes, him, woman. I said "your husband."—Do you understand that word? My friend, your husband, the honest, honest Iago.

EMILIA

If he said that, then I hope his malicious soul rots in hell forever. He's lying through his teeth! She was too attached to her filthy marriage ever to do a thing like that!

OTHELLO *draws his sword.*

OTHELLO

Ha!

EMILIA

Go ahead, do your worst. Killing me won't send you to heaven. You weren't good enough for her.

OTHELLO

You'd better shut up!

EMILIA

I can endure far more pain than you could ever give me! Oh, you idiot! You stupid fool! As dumb as dirt! You've committed a terrible evil—I'm not afraid of your sword. I'll tell everyone what you did, even if it

Though I lost twenty lives.—Help! Help, ho! Help!
180   The Moor hath killed my mistress! Murder, murder!

Enter MONTANO, GRATIANO, *and* IAGO

MONTANO
What is the matter? How now, general?

EMILIA
Oh, are you come, Iago? You have done well,
That men must lay their murders on your neck.

GRATIANO
What is the matter?

EMILIA
185   *(to* IAGO*)* Disprove this villain, if thou be'st a man.
He says thou told'st him that his wife was false.
I know thou didst not, thou'rt not such a villain.
Speak, for my heart is full.

IAGO
I told him what I thought, and told no more
190   Than what he found himself was apt and true.

EMILIA
But did you ever tell him she was false?

IAGO
I did.

EMILIA
You told a lie, an odious, damnèd lie.
Upon my soul, a lie, a wicked lie.
195   She false with Cassio! Did you say with Cassio?

IAGO
With Cassio, mistress. Go to, charm your tongue.

EMILIA
I will not charm my tongue, I am bound to speak.
My mistress here lies murdered in her bed—

ALL
Oh, heavens forfend!

costs me my life twenty times over.—Help, help, help! The Moor's killed my mistress! Murder, murder!

MONTANO, GRATIANO, and IAGO enter.

MONTANO

What's the matter? What's going on here, general?

EMILIA

Oh, are you here, Iago? You've done a good job, that other men can attribute their murders to you!

GRATIANO

What's the matter?

EMILIA

(to IAGO) Tell this villain he's wrong, if you're man enough. He says you told him his wife cheated on him. I know you didn't. You're not that much of a villain. Speak, because I'm too emotional to say any more.

IAGO

I told him what I thought. I didn't tell him anything that didn't make sense or ring true to him.

EMILIA

But did you tell him she cheated on him?

IAGO

I did.

EMILIA

Then you told a lie, a sick, wicked lie. I swear on my soul it was a lie. You said she slept with Cassio. Did you say Cassio?

IAGO

Yes, with Cassio. Now be quiet.

EMILIA

I will not be quiet! I have to speak. My mistress here lies murdered in her bed—

ALL

No, heaven forbid!

EMILIA

200   And your reports have set the murder on.

OTHELLO

Nay, stare not, masters, it is true, indeed.

GRATIANO

'Tis a strange truth.

MONTANO

Oh, monstrous act!

EMILIA

Villainy, villainy, villainy!
I think upon 't, I think I smell 't, Oh, villainy!
205   I thought so then, I'll kill myself for grief.
Oh, villainy, villainy!

IAGO

What, are you mad? I charge you, get you home.

EMILIA

Good gentlemen, let me have leave to speak.
'Tis proper I obey him, but not now.
210   Perchance, Iago, I will ne'er go home.

OTHELLO

Oh! Oh! Oh!

EMILIA

Nay, lay thee down and roar,
For thou hast killed the sweetest innocent
That e'er did lift up eye.

OTHELLO

Oh, she was foul!—
I scarce did know you, uncle. There lies your niece,
215   Whose breath, indeed, these hands have newly stopped.
I know this act shows horrible and grim.

GRATIANO

Poor Desdemon! I am glad thy father's dead,
Thy match was mortal to him, and pure grief
Shore his old thread in twain. Did he live now,

EMILIA

And your lies caused this murder.

OTHELLO

Don't stand there gaping, everyone. It's true.

GRATIANO

It may be true, but it's unbelievable.

MONTANO

Oh, what a horrible deed!

EMILIA

Evil, evil, evil! I can smell it! I suspected it earlier. I'll kill myself out of grief! Oh, evil, evil!

IAGO

Are you crazy? I'm ordering you, go home.

EMILIA

Good gentlemen, give me permission to speak. I know I ought to obey my husband, but not now. Maybe I'll never go home again, Iago!

OTHELLO

Oh! Oh! Oh!

EMILIA

Yes, go ahead and moan, because you killed the sweetest, most innocent woman who ever lived!

OTHELLO

Gratiano is Brabantio's brother and Desdemona's uncle.

She was filthy! I barely knew you, Uncle Gratiano. Here's your niece lying here dead. I killed her with these hands. I know this looks horrible.

GRATIANO

Poor Desdemona! I'm glad your father isn't alive to see this. Your marriage made him die of grief before his time. If he was alive now, this sight would hurt him

220   This sight would make him do a desperate turn,
    Yea, curse his better angel from his side
    And fall to reprobation.

OTHELLO
    'Tis pitiful, but yet Iago knows
    That she with Cassio hath the act of shame
225   A thousand times committed. Cassio confessed it,
    And she did gratify his amorous works
    With that recognizance and pledge of love
    Which I first gave her. I saw it in his hand,
    It was a handkerchief, an antique token
230   My father gave my mother.

EMILIA
                      Oh, heaven! Oh, heavenly powers!

IAGO
    Zounds, hold your peace.

EMILIA
    'Twill out, 'twill out.—I peace?
    No, I will speak as liberal as the north.
    Let heaven and men and devils, let them all,
235   All, all cry shame against me, yet I'll speak.

IAGO
    Be wise, and get you home.

Draws his sword

EMILIA
    I will not.

GRATIANO
    Fie! Your sword upon a woman?

EMILIA
    O thou dull Moor! That handkerchief thou speak'st of
240   I found by fortune and did give my husband.
    For often, with a solemn earnestness—
    More than indeed belonged to such a trifle—
    He begged of me to steal it.

terribly. It would make him curse the heavens and be damned to hell.

OTHELLO

It's sad, but Iago knows she had sex with Cassio a thousand times. Cassio confessed it, and she pledged her love to him by giving him the handkerchief I'd given her. I saw it in his hand.

It was an old memento that my father gave to my mother.

EMILIA

Oh, God! Dear God in heaven!

IAGO

Damn it, shut your mouth.

EMILIA

No, the truth will come out—Me, shut my mouth? Let heaven and men and devils tell me to shut me up. I'll say what I have to say.

IAGO

If you're smart, you'll go home.

IAGO *draws his sword.*

EMILIA

I won't.

GRATIANO

Shame on you! Drawing your sword on a woman?

EMILIA

Oh, you stupid Moor! I found that handkerchief by accident and gave it to my husband. He'd begged me to steal it many times.

IAGO

                                        Villainous whore!

EMILIA

She give it Cassio? No, alas, I found it
245   And I did give 't my husband.

IAGO

                                        Filth, thou liest!

EMILIA

By heaven, I do not, I do not, gentlemen.—
(to OTHELLO*)*
O murderous coxcomb! What should such a fool
Do with so good a wife?

OTHELLO

                                Are there no stones in heaven
But what serve for the thunder?—Precious villain!

He runs at IAGO
IAGO *stabs* EMILIA

GRATIANO

250   The woman falls! Sure he hath killed his wife.

EMILIA

Ay, ay. Oh, lay me by my mistress' side.

                                        Exit IAGO

GRATIANO

He's gone, but his wife's killed.

MONTANO

'Tis a notorious villain. Take you this weapon,
Which I have recovered from the Moor.
255   Come, guard the door without. Let him not pass,
But kill him rather. I'll after that same villain,
For 'tis a damnèd slave.

                                Exeunt MONTANO *and* GRATIANO

IAGO

You evil whore!

EMILIA

You think she gave it to Cassio? No, I found it and gave it to my husband.

IAGO

You piece of filth, you're lying!

EMILIA

I swear I'm not lying. *(to* OTHELLO*)* Oh, you murderous fool! How did you ever get such a good wife?

OTHELLO

Won't heaven strike this Iago dead? You absolute villain!

OTHELLO *runs at* IAGO. IAGO *stabs* EMILIA.

GRATIANO

The woman's falling down! He's killed his wife!

EMILIA

Yes, yes! Lay me next to my mistress.

IAGO *exits.*

GRATIANO

He's gone, and his wife's dead.

MONTANO

He's a wicked, horrible criminal. Take the Moor's sword and guard the door from the outside. Kill him rather than let him leave this room. I'm going after Iago. He's a horrid criminal.

MONTANO *and* GRATIANO *exit.*

OTHELLO

                    I am not valiant neither,
But ever puny whipster gets my sword.
But why should honor outlive honesty?

260   Let it go all.

EMILIA

             What did thy song bode, lady?
Hark, canst thou hear me? I will play the swan.
And die in music.
(singing)   *Willow, willow, willow—*

Moor, she was chaste, she loved thee, cruel Moor.
So come my soul to bliss, as I speak true.

265   So speaking as I think, alas, I die.

Dies

OTHELLO

    I have another weapon in this chamber,
It was a sword of Spain, the ice-brook's temper.
Oh, here it is. Uncle, I must come forth.

GRATIANO

    (within) If thou attempt it, it will cost thee dear.

270   Thou hast no weapon, and perforce must suffer.

OTHELLO

    Look in upon me then and speak with me,
Or, naked as I am, I will assault thee.

Enter GRATIANO

GRATIANO

    What is the matter?

OTHELLO

              Behold, I have a weapon.
A better never did itself sustain

275   Upon a soldier's thigh. I have seen the day

OTHELLO

I'm not that strong, if a puny nobody can grab my sword. But why should my reputation for honor last longer than my honor did? Let it all go.

EMILIA

What did your song mean, lady? Can you hear me? I'll die like a swan. They sing when they die.
(singing) Willow, willow, willow.—
Moor, she never cheated on you. She loved you, you cruel man. I swear on my soul I'm telling the truth, and as I say this, I die.

EMILIA dies.

OTHELLO

I've got another weapon in the room. It's a Spanish sword, hardened in ice cold water and razor sharp. Here it is. Uncle, I'm coming out!

GRATIANO

(offstage) If you try that, you'll pay for it. You've got no weapon, so you'll have to suffer.

OTHELLO

Look in on me, and talk with me, or I'll attack even without a weapon.

GRATIANO enters.

GRATIANO

What's the matter?

OTHELLO

Look, I have a weapon, the best sword a soldier could have. I've fought my way through obstacles twenty times more terrifying than you with this weapon. But

That with this little arm and this good sword
I have made my way through more impediments
Than twenty times your stop. But, oh, vain boast!
Who can control his fate? 'tis not so now.

280 Be not afraid, though you do see me weaponed.
Here is my journey's end, here is my butt,
And very sea-mark of my utmost sail.
Do you go back dismayed? 'tis a lost fear.
Man but a rush against Othello's breast,

285 And he retires. Where should Othello go?—
Now, how dost thou look now? O ill-starred wench,
Pale as thy smock! When we shall meet at compt
This look of thine will hurl my soul from heaven
And fiends will snatch at it. Cold, cold, my girl,

290 Even like thy chastity. O cursed, cursed slave!
Whip me, ye devils,
From the possession of this heavenly sight!
Blow me about in winds, roast me in sulfur,
Wash me in steep-down gulfs of liquid fire!—

295 Oh, Desdemona! Desdemona! dead! Oh! Oh!

Enter LODOVICO, MONTANO, CASSIO *carried in a chair,
and officers with* IAGO, *prisoner*

LODOVICO
Where is this rash and most unfortunate man?

OTHELLO
That's he that was Othello. Here I am.

LODOVICO
Where is that viper? Bring the villain forth.

IAGO *is brought forward*

who can control his fate? I'm not like that now. Don't be afraid, even though you see me with a weapon. This is the end of my journey, the end of my life. Are you backing away in fear? There's no reason to be afraid. You could tap me with a feather and I'd back away. Where would Othello go?—Oh, look at you! Such cruel luck! You're as pale as your nightgown! When we meet on Judgment Day, that look of yours will send me from heaven to hell, where devils will grab me. You're cold, cold, and you were never hot with lust. Oh you damned villain! Whip me, you devils, so I don't have to look at this heavenly sight! Blow on me with hot winds, roast me in lava, drown me in liquid fire! Oh, Desdemona! Dead Desdemona! Oh, oh!

LODOVICO *and* MONTANO *enter, followed by* CASSIO *on a stretcher, and officers with* IAGO, *prisoner.*

LODOVICO

Where is that poor rash man?

OTHELLO

You mean the man who used to be Othello? Here I am.

LODOVICO

Where's that snake? Bring the villain forward.

IAGO *is brought forward.*

OTHELLO
I look down towards his feet, but that's a fable.
300   If that thou be'st a devil, I cannot kill thee.

Stabs IAGO

LODOVICO
Wrench his sword from him.

They take OTHELLO*'s sword*

IAGO
I bleed, sir, but not killed.

OTHELLO
I am not sorry neither. I'd have thee live,
For in my sense 'tis happiness to die.

LODOVICO
O thou Othello, thou was once so good,
305   Fall'n in the practice of a cursèd slave,
What shall be said to thee?

OTHELLO
Why, anything.
An honorable murderer, if you will,
For naught I did in hate, but all in honor.

LODOVICO
This wretch hath part confessed his villainy.
310   Did you and he consent in Cassio's death?

OTHELLO
Ay.

CASSIO
Dear general, I never gave you cause.

OTHELLO
I do believe it, and I ask your pardon.
Will you, I pray, demand that demi-devil
315   Why he hath thus ensnared my soul and body?

OTHELLO

I'm looking to see if you have cloven hooves like the devil. But that's just a fairy tale. If you are a devil, I won't be able to kill you.

OTHELLO *stabs* IAGO.

LODOVICO

Take his sword away from him.

They take OTHELLO*'s sword away.*

IAGO

I'm bleeding, but you didn't kill me.

OTHELLO

I'm not sorry, either. I want you to live, since to me, death is happiness.

LODOVICO

Oh Othello, you were once so good, then you were tricked by this villain. What can I say to you?

OTHELLO

Say anything. Call me an honorable murderer if you like. I did nothing out of hate, only out of honor.

LODOVICO

This poor guy's partly confessed his plan. Did you plan Cassio's death with him?

OTHELLO

Yes.

CASSIO

Dear general, I never gave you any reason to hate me.

OTHELLO

I believe you, and I ask you to forgive me. Will you please make this half-devil say why he tricked me and damned my soul?

IAGO

Demand me nothing. What you know, you know.
From this time forth I never will speak word.

LODOVICO

What, not to pray?

GRATIANO

Torments will ope your lips.

OTHELLO

320   Well, thou dost best.

LODOVICO

Sir, you shall understand what hath befall'n,
Which, as I think, you know not. Here is a letter
Found in the pocket of the slain Roderigo,
And here another. The one of them imports
325   The death of Cassio to be undertook
By Roderigo.

OTHELLO

Oh, villain!

CASSIO

Most heathenish and most gross!

LODOVICO

Now here's another discontented paper
330   Found in his pocket too, and this, it seems,
Roderigo meant to have sent this damnèd villain
But that, belike, Iago in the interim
Came in and satisfied him.

OTHELLO

O thou pernicious caitiff!
335   How came you, Cassio, by that handkerchief
That was my wife's?

CASSIO

                                        I found it in my chamber,
And he himself confessed but even now
That there he dropped it for a special purpose
Which wrought to his desire.

IAGO

Don't ask me anything. You know what you know. From this moment on, I'll never say another word.

LODOVICO

What, not even to pray?

GRATIANO

Torture will make you talk.

OTHELLO

Well, do your best.

LODOVICO

Sir, you'll understand everything that has happened. I don't think you know now. Here is a letter we found in Roderigo's pocket. And here's another. This one talks about how Roderigo should kill Cassio.

OTHELLO

Oh, you villain!

CASSIO

Ungodly and monstrous!

LODOVICO

Here's another letter from his pocket, addressed to Iago and full of complaints. We think he was going to send it to Iago, but then Iago stepped in and answered his complaints by killing him.

OTHELLO

Oh, you wicked scoundrel! Cassio, how did you get my wife's handkerchief?

CASSIO

I found it in my room, and Iago just confessed that he put it there for his own purposes.

OTHELLO
                                   O fool! fool! fool!

CASSIO
340   There is besides in Roderigo's letter
        How he upbraids Iago, that he made him
        Brave me upon the watch, whereon it came
        That I was cast. And even but now he spake,
        After long seeming dead—Iago hurt him,
345   Iago set him on.

LODOVICO
        (to OTHELLO) You must forsake this room and go with us.
        Your power and your command is taken off
        And Cassio rules in Cyprus. For this slave,
        If there be any cunning cruelty
350   That can torment him much and hold him long,
        It shall be his. You shall close prisoner rest
        Till that the nature of your fault be known
        To the Venetian state.—Come, bring him away.

OTHELLO
        Soft you, a word or two before you go.
355   I have done the state some service, and they know 't.
        No more of that. I pray you, in your letters,
        When you shall these unlucky deeds relate,
        Speak of me as I am. Nothing extenuate,
        Nor set down aught in malice. Then must you speak
360   Of one that loved not wisely, but too well.
        Of one not easily jealous, but being wrought,
        Perplexed in the extreme. Of one whose hand,
        Like the base Indian, threw a pearl away
        Richer than all his tribe. Of one whose subdued eyes,
365   Albeit unused to the melting mood,
        Drop tears as fast as the Arabian trees
        Their medicinal gum. Set you down this,

OTHELLO

Oh, what a fool I am!

CASSIO

Also, in his letter to Iago, Roderigo criticizes Iago for telling him to get me angry while I was on guard duty, and get me demoted. And just now he admitted it, even though he'd seemed to be dead for a long while— Iago tricked him, Iago urged him to do it.

LODOVICO

(to OTHELLO) You'll have to leave this room and come with us. You're stripped of your power and your command, and Cassio will govern Cyprus. As for this slave, Iago, if we can think of any torture that will hurt him a lot but keep him alive a long time, he'll have it. You'll remain a prisoner until we bring your crimes to the Venetian government.—Okay, take him away.

OTHELLO

Wait. A word or two before you go. I've given the state of Venice a bit of help in the past, and they know it. But enough about that. When you record these sad events in your letters, please describe me exactly as I am. Don't tone things down or exaggerate them out of hostility. If you're being fair, you'll have to describe me as someone who loved too much, but who wasn't wise about it. I was not easily made jealous, but once I was tricked and manipulated, I worked myself into a frenzy. Describe me as a fool who threw away a precious pearl with his own hands, like a silly Indian who didn't know what it was worth. As someone who was not emotional, but who then cried a lot. Write all this

And say besides that in Aleppo once,
Where a malignant and a turbaned Turk
370 Beat a Venetian and traduced the state,
I took by the throat the circumcisèd dog,
And smote him, thus.

Stabs himself

LODOVICO
Oh, bloody period!

GRATIANO
All that is spoke is marred.

OTHELLO
(*to* **DESDEMONA**)
375 I kissed thee ere I killed thee. No way but this,
Killing myself, to die upon a kiss.

Kisses **DESDEMONA**, *dies*

CASSIO
This did I fear, but thought he had no weapon,
For he was great of heart.

LODOVICO
(*to* **IAGO**)
                                    O Spartan dog,
More fell than anguish, hunger, or the sea,
380 Look on the tragic loading of this bed.
This is thy work. The object poisons sight,
Let it be hid.—Gratiano, keep the house
And seize upon the fortunes of the Moor,
For they succeed on you.—To you, lord governor,
385 Remains the censure of this hellish villain:
The time, the place, the torture. Oh, enforce it!
Myself will straight aboard, and to the state
This heavy act with heavy heart relate.

Exeunt